Worlds of Fear

By

@TheQuillsTip

First paperback edition June 2018

ISBN 978-0-9837999-1-7 (paperback)

ISBN 978-0-9837999-2-4 (ebook)

www.TheQuillsTip.com

I dedicate this book to all the lonely words in the world that have yet to find a place to truly call home.

As well, I dedicate this book to Bankhead Bistro & Corporal Ray's Coffee Shop in Aledo, Texas. Thank you for all the mochas and for allowing me to linger for many hours.

Lastly, but certainly not least, I dedicate this book to my wife and children who have stood by, encouraged and inspired me to finish this feat. You all have been a well of support from which I continually draw. For this I am truly indebted to you all forever.

Life Begins at the Quill's Tip

Table of Contents

Introduction 1

Chapter 1- The Battles Begin 3

Chapter 2 - Devastating News.................................... 19

Chapter 3 - The Jungle Calls 25

Chapter 4 - The Fog of War....................................... 55

Chapter 5 - Operation Unplanned Rescue 82

Chapter 6 - Time Marches On 112

Chapter 7 - The Castle in the Mountain 117

Chapter 8 - A Plea for Help....................................... 132

Chapter 9 - The Impending Battle............................... 142

Chapter 10 - Expecting the Unexpected........................ 156

Chapter 11 - Internality Revealed 173

Chapter 12 - Unmasking Fear 181

Introduction

For many people fear can be their greatest foe. For James L'Beau it certainly is. Ever since his father passed away, when he was only five years old, fear has taken a tight grasp on his mind. And now that he is an adult, the unknown future is his dread.

Every person faces some measure of fear each day, and each day, they deal with it in their own way. But James L'Beau's way is extraordinarily unique: he turns within to a whole other world! Through the years, Jim has been able to create his own fantasy world to battle his arch nemesis: *Fobos*, the ruler of his fear.

When Jim finds himself confronted with a measure of fear which he cannot handle, he feels almost as if he is going to implode. It is at this very moment that instead of imploding, he turns within and finds himself in the midst of an entirely different reality. Each time Jim turns within, he discovers a new surrounding, a new time and place, struggling with all his wit and might to combat. But no matter the time and setting the enemy is always the same - *Fobos*.

To a certain extent, Jim always manages to keep Fobos at bay, leaving their battles a stalemate. However, it is clear that Fobos is in charge, not Jim, because Jim is always fighting his enemy, never defeating him. This ongoing battle against Fobos is bitter-sweet to Jim because on the one hand he loves discovering new places each time he turns within, while on the other hand, this incessant battle has worn him down over the years. As well, it has alienated him from many friends and family, because they simply cannot understand his struggle (not that they would believe him if he told them). Unbeknownst to Jim though, this perpetual stalemate will soon end, and one of them will finally gain the upper-hand.

Chapter 1- The Battles Begin

Today is a fateful day for James Frederich L'Beau. The problem is he does not yet know it. Soon enough he will know it, but will it be in time? He is like most of us; traipsing through the jungle of life, not realizing there is a pool of quicksand just beyond the next bush or tree until we are up to our neck in it.

James, or Jim, as everyone affectionately calls him, is a sophomore at the University of Chicago, where he received a full academic scholarship. Observing the help his attorney stepfather offered to so many as Jim was growing up, he felt intrigued by the wide realm of government and the law. Although Jim is not quite sure he wants to be an attorney himself, he is studying Political Science because of his long-held admiration of his stepfather's career.

He is very excited, because the start of his sophomore year marked the beginning of Jim actually working toward his major, now that he has jumped through all the general studies hoops. This means that Jim is now a frequent guest at the *Joseph Regenstein Library*, where he spends many hours parsing through multiple textbook and history books.

Jim has a place he frequents for dinner, called the *57th Street Grill*. It is a nice little joint, where he can grab a hamburger to eat and look out over the beach and take in Lake Michigan at sunset. Most of the time he doesn't eat alone, but joins his girlfriend Lauren there. Today is their weekly date night. They both appreciate the break, because it is a respite from their arduous school schedules; however, this night, although it would be memorable, it would be so for all the wrong reasons.

Lauren meets him near the north side of the library at 5:30 just as they had planned, and they make their way east on 56th Street. She shares her whole morning story of how she woke up late because she forgot to set her alarm clock, which led to her forgetting her homework, which led to her not being able to turn it in on time, which led to her getting her grade automatically docked. This was *no bueno* for sure. Regardless of how the morning started, her afternoon turns out to be quite the opposite, as she strolls the street, arm in arm with her handsome beau.

As they converse, they near an intersection at South Lake Park Avenue, and neither Jim nor Lauren pay much attention, since they have made this trip on numerous occasions. The street is on their right and there is a wall on their left. Lauren walks on Jim's left side, and as they come to the intersection, a man lunges at Lauren's purse. He has a knife and cuts the purse strap very quickly. Lauren screams at the top of her lungs, and Jim pulls her toward himself while simultaneously stepping towards the man although he is not sure what he is going to do against this knife-wielding thief.

This startling event unfolds so quickly and so unexpectedly that there is no time to make rational decisions. The robber timed this perfectly. A bus which stopped to let off passengers is about to take off when the man slips aboard just as the door closes. Jim makes a quick dash to chase the man, but as the bus driver pulls forward, apparently he does not see Jim. At that moment the world shrinks to slow motion for Jim. He sees the bus pulling away, he hears Lauren screaming behind him, and he feels himself tripping on the curb in his panicked sprint. He realizes this situation is about to go from bad to worse, because he is about to collide with this bus (or the bus with him). Either way, it ain't good.

Just before he and the bus physically greet one another, Jim's heart seizes with fear, not knowing if he is about to meet his maker. "Aaggghhhh!" he yells, as he braces for impact. Time seems to slow to the speed of molasses, and he sees himself falling to the ground. Yet, when he glances up, just before he smashes into the bus, he realizes that instead of falling to the road, he is falling from a horse. In that nanosecond, he thinks to himself, "Oh no! Here we go again!"

****

Within a breath's moment of him hitting the ground, a group of men, completely clad in metallic armor surround Jim with shouts of consternation, "Your Majesty, are you okay?"

Jim lay on his back, staring up into the clear blue sky, the golden-orbed sun shining brightly on his face.

Did they just call me, 'Your Majesty?' "Where am I?" he wondered. "*Where is Lauren? Is she alright?*"

These questions will be answered soon enough, but not now. First, some explanations are in order.

****

What led up to this point for James Frederich L'Beau?

I am glad you ask, because if our stage is not properly set, you will not be able to fully grasp the entire scope of Jim's predicament, now will you? So, put on your best walking shoes, and take a stroll with me down memory lane. Not our own memories, of course, but that of Jim's. Oh, don't worry, we'll have you back in time for supper. That is, if you are a voracious reader.

You see, for James L'Beau, his tale began in a quaint little farm town in Wisconsin called Delavan. He is the baby out of the three children, born to Lawrence & Anel L'Beau. In 1975, when James was only five years old, his father suddenly passed away with heart failure, leaving Anel, at the age of thirty, a widow with three children. Jim was still very young at the time, so he did not remember every detail surrounding his father's death. However, despite his young age at the time, the image of his motionless father slumped over his desk was seared into his memory. Just a short time after this tragedy, Jim would have the first encounter with unbearable fear, and it was during this time that he took his first journey *inward*.

Because Jim's father died, his mom worked the second shift at a nursing home which left the children on many nights to fend for themselves. Jim's sister, Theresa, was 10, and his brother, John, was 11, so they were tasked with watching over him at night. Even though they fought like cats and dogs much of the time, they usually took great care of their baby brother. But no matter how well Jim was taken care of by them (or his mother), it did not halt the fear he would encounter from encroaching upon his very soul. And it is within his soul that Jim engages in mortal combat for many years.

From an early age, Jim loved to read books and have them read to him. He especially loved to hear tales of yesteryear filled with adventure and vivid descriptions of ancient civilizations. Little did he know that these stories would, through the years, serve as the backdrop for his battles against his archnemesis Fobos.

Exactly one year after his father passed away, it was an especially hard day for his mother, because she dearly missed her husband. She cried most of the day as she sat staring out the window. Jim felt helpless to console his mother during these times, so he often just retreated to his room. That particular day was no different. However, instead of playing with his toys as usual, Jim, emotionally drained, decided to take a nap. He grabbed a book on pirates to look through as he lay in bed until he fell asleep. When he awoke, he found himself completely alone.

He frantically searched the house inside and out, looking for his brother and sister, yelling desperately for them, "Theresa! John! Where are you?" But they were nowhere to be found. He knew that his mother was at work, so he could handle that. But being alone at six years old he could not handle.

After their mother left for work, Theresa and John realized that Jim was still asleep, so they had decided to sneak out to their friend's house next door. Their tween brains didn't dwell on how long Jim might sleep, but just figured it was plenty of time to hang out with their friends and make it back in time to fix supper for him. Oh, how they were wrong.

Jim now realized that no one was in the house but himself. But the more he pondered this fact, the more he became paralyzed with fear. Giving up on his frantic search, he slid to the floor in the corner of their living room, not knowing what to do, and tears began to pour forth uncontrollably. For the first time in his life Jim was alone, and this absolutely terrified him. If ever there was a living, breathing example of human terror, he was it.

As he sat staring out into the dimly lit room, all of a sudden the walls, the floor, and the ceiling began to languidly shift and move. It was as if they were melting into putty and before Jim realized it; his house was no longer his house.

Before he could ascertain his whereabouts, though, a gush of ocean water crashed into his face.

"Don't just stand there, get up that rigging, laddie!" cried Jean Blanc, First Mate.

Jim was on board *Hermes*, an old sailing ship; triple-masted, double decks, and carrying forty guns (twenty guns per deck). It seemed like an eternity since that initial dose of salty water hit him in the face, and he felt disconnected from his new and astonishing surroundings. Time seemed to stand still. A second wave splashed him, jarring his senses once again.

Jean Blanc yelled again from the helm, "You land-lover, get yer chicken legs up that riggin', and tie down that sail, boy!"

This yell jolted Jim into at least some cognitive state of mind, and now he knew this man, whoever he might be, was *indeed* yelling at him. It was a strange feeling because Jim knew he was not at home, yet there was no fear of his new surroundings. Chaotic peace seemed to envelop him.

At once, Jim began his ascent up the forty-foot rigging mast, climbing from one rope rung to the next, all the way up the netted ladder. He reached the insubordinate rope, and immediately tied the sail down. How he knew how to do it was unbeknownst to him, for he had never sailed a day in his life, let alone tied off a sail rigging. But handling that rope felt as if he had done it a thousand times before. After Jim fixed the sail, though, he could not help but take in the vista from the height where he now stood.

All he could see for miles and miles was dark-blue ocean. The sky was partially cloudy, but the sun still managed to burst through with spots here and there on the face of the water. There was a slight breeze running through Jim's hair, and the smell of salt water permeated the air. A couple flocks of geese could be seen in the distance, making their way north as the grip of winter loosened. Jim also spotted a group of dolphins bobbing in and out of the water, as they nonchalantly mastered the upper echelon of that great pool called the ocean. Everything seemed so peaceful and like a delicious cup of sweet ice tea on a hot summer's day, he drank it all in.

The scene was breathtaking, and Jim wanted to just watch and soak it all in. But the Captain thought otherwise.

"Now get back down here, laddie!"

So just as quickly as Jim ascended the mast, he descended it. As soon as his feet touched the deck of the ship, he knew that something was awry. Everyone on the ship seemed to be frantically scurrying from one place to another, as if they knew something that he did not. He certainly felt like the odd man out.

As Gustav, one of the crew, went bustling by, Jim caught him by the arm and asked, "What's with all the commotion?"

Gustav looked at Jim with a confused look, and said, "Don't you know that we are preparing for battle?"

"Battle?" said Jim. "A battle with who?" he asked.

"We've been trying to outrun Captain Fobos and his band of thieves for over a day now, but they're gainin' on us. So, Cap'n ordered us to prepare for battle before nightfall. Did you hit your head or sommin'?" questioned Gustav. Then Gustav took off in a frenzy.

At this point Jim was rather disconcerted to say the least, so he figured he would try and speak with the captain. Jim saw him standing off to the side of the steersman, pouring over maps of the area. He ran up the stairs to the quarter deck, and quickly approached him. Jim tugged on his shirt, "Captain, are we really preparing for battle?"

"Most certainly, laddie! Fobos is less than a day behind us, and he will catch up to us by mornin', if not sooner," Captain Dojure explained.

"What do you want me to do?" asked Jim.

"Stay by me, laddie. No matter what happens, stay by me," Captain Dojure told Jim in a reassuring manner.

Jim watched as the crew finished the final preparations for battle, and then the cook's crew took turns bringing around food for everyone. Jim took a little to eat, and so did the Captain. Having some food in his stomach brought a measure of comfort for Jim, but he was still somewhat unnerved with the thought of an impending battle. There would be no sleep tonight!

Once the sun set, everyone rested (or at least tried to). Men were strewn out on the deck with guns. The crews manning the cannons were all sitting huddled together with their backs against the cannon trying to catch a little shuteye. The men in the crow's nest kept a watchful eye out for Captain Fobos' ship, but it was becoming increasingly difficult with the fog that rolled in.

Jim sat on a bench, which was just outside the Captain's quarters, watching Captain Dojure as he manned the steering wheel, but at some point Jim fell asleep from the slow rock of the ship and the heavy weight of night. He was only asleep for what seemed like minutes, when the call from the crow's nest rang out, "Fobos sighted!" The entire crew, including Jim, sprang to life, and once again, there was a frantic scene on deck, like cockroaches scattering at the flip of a light switch.

Captain Dojure was no longer at the wheel, but, instead, he handed it off to the first mate, Jean Blanc. The captain was checking over all the gun stations to make sure his crew was indeed ready for the battle. Once Jim located him on the deck, he quickly made his way towards him, because he remembered the words of the captain, "Stay by me, laddie. No matter what happens, stay by me."

When he reached him, Jim was like a fawn to its mother, looking to Dojure for his every direction. Fobos and his crew were within an hour's time from their ship. They could see their lanterns in the dark night. Fobos' ship was bigger and faster, so Dojure's ship had no chance of outrunning it. The pirates would have caught them sooner had there not been a storm three nights previously, and Dojure thought they had outwitted them by turning off their normal course. Obviously they had not.

Everyone was as ready as they could be, knowing that death was most certainly imminent for some, if not for all in their crew. Fobos' ship and crew were notorious for attacking ships up and down the eastern coast of Africa, and up until then, no one with a bigger, faster ship than he had been able to catch them and bring them to justice. They always managed to attack and slip away at just the right moments, as if their old ship magically possessed radar. This was one of those ripe moments to attack – a merchant ship, which was much smaller than theirs and would most certainly be carrying valuable cargo, was sailing alone!

Jim knew that he was on a sailing ship in the middle of the ocean with a battle against a pirate ship impending, yet at that same moment he was also cognizant that he was from Delavan, Wisconsin. He could see his house in his mind, and could see himself sitting there in the corner of his living room, frightened from being alone. As if he were holding a diamond in his very hand, he could completely see the different facets of the situation he was now in, but at the same time he was not frightened. Somehow, being beside Captain Dojure brought Jim a measure of peace.

After the Captain checked over the entire crew, he returned to the quarter deck with Jim in tow. The enemy would reach them within the half hour, and the battle would take place. There was no way around it. Captain Dojure turned to Jim and handed him a small sword. At that very moment Jim remembered the story of the *Hobbit*, and knew exactly how Bilbo Baggins must have felt, when he first received that ancient elvish blade from Gandalf.

"You'll need this, laddie," the Captain said. "Are you scared?"

"A little," Jim replied.

"That's okay, laddie. I was too before me first battle!" Captain Dojure said in a reassuring manner.

Within a short time, Fobos and his ship were finally within cannon range, so Captain Dojure ordered for the guns to open fire. Boom…boom…boom…boom! The guns shook Jim to the core, because he did not expect them to be so loud. Actually he did not really know what to expect at all. Captain Dojure and his crew had been trying their best to make it to the nearest island. There they knew that they had a chance to out maneuver Fobos and his crew, since his ship was much larger. But they ran up against a strong head wind, which slowed them down. Fobos was coming towards their starboard side, and his crew returned fire at Dojure's ship.

As the battle began, it started to rain. It was not pouring down, but it was a steady drizzle, which made things even more miserable. The two ships continued to exchange fire, and each ship caused considerable damage to the other. The cannon fire worked like wrecking balls tearing into an old wooden building being demolished. Soon Fobos' ship slammed into *Hermes*, like ants attacking dropped food on the ground, but they were met with fierce resistance from Captain Dojure and his men. Jim found himself clutching Captain Dojure's shirt from behind as he helped by swinging his sword when he could. In the midst of the fighting Jim strained to try and catch a glimpse of Fobos. He saw Fobos from some distance but his face was covered with some sort of mask. For some reason Jim felt let down by not seeing the face of their enemy.

Captain Dojure and his men would not be defeated easily, but he knew the inevitable outcome would soon overtake him and his men. As they bravely fought, Captain Dojure gave the order, "Abandon ship!" This was the code for the men in the magazine to light a timed-fuse, so that all of Dojure's men had enough time to jump ship before the explosion took them out as well.

Grabbing anything and everything within reach that could float, the captain and his men dove into the dreary ocean. Jim was still right in tow behind Captain Dojure, and they jumped overboard together. Most of his crew were either killed or lost at sea, but some managed to escape. They had lowered their lifeboats before Fobos caught up with them, just in case they needed to escape, and it was a good thing that Dojure ordered them to do this.

Once they were in the lifeboats, they rowed as fast as they could to get away from the blast that was soon to hit the enemy from within their own ship. They had only rowed for two or three minutes, when they could hear, see, and feel the concussion from the blast. *Kaaa-boooooooom!* The blast not only split Captain Dojure's ship in half, but it blew an irreparable hole into Fobos' ship as well. They may have lost *Hermes* to Fobos, but Fobos had lost his ship to them.

Captain Dojure and his men rowed frantically for the island they had tried to reach earlier, because they knew that if Fobos and his men had any lifeboats of their own they would be after them for sure. These pirates were like ravenous wolves, unceasingly tracking their prey. The rain was now pouring down and even though Jim had survived his first battle intact with Captain Dojure, he was miserable now. The men rowed so vigorously and the rain poured down so hard that they could not see how quickly they approached land. Before they knew it, the waves slammed their lifeboats into the jagged rocks edging the shore, sending the crew flying into the water.

As soon as Jim hit the water, he blacked out.

"Jim! Jim! Wake up, wake up!!" cried the distant, muffled voices.

Jim awoke and slowly sat up. As he did, he turned over, spewing water and seaweed from his mouth. He was back in his own house, still sitting in the same corner of the living room, but now his brother and sister were there with him.

"Jim, are you alright?" Theresa asked breathlessly, as they both knelt over him.

"Jim, why are you soaking wet?" John questioned.

Jim was soaking wet from head to toe, reeking with the smell of saltwater.

John and Theresa helped him to his feet, and Jim stumbled to the shower to wash off the saltwater. It was such a bizarre situation, they couldn't relate to it. They didn't ask too many questions, because they knew if their mom found out they would be in serious trouble for leaving their brother home alone. Theresa and John reckoned it was better to not know what happened than to risk Jim telling on them. They just set about putting things in order again. After Jim dried off and changed, Theresa threw Jim's clothes in the dryer while John cleaned up Jim's water-seaweed mess and fixed him something to eat for dinner.

"It had only been a dream, right?" Jim thought to himself as he ate his dinner. His stomach rumbled, but the very normal act of eating dinner seemed crazy after fighting with pirates. *"Why did I wake up in my house soaked in saltwater and spitting up seaweed?"* he wondered. On top of these questions, the issue of time plagued Jim's thoughts. According to his brother and sister, they were only gone for an hour or two, but Jim was on that ship and in that battle for over half a day! This experience took Jim completely by surprise, and now he had no idea how to cope with it. He was not even sure that he *did* want to cope with it.

He suddenly realized that this could be the beginning of a very useful tool in his life, because he now began to wonder if he could go to this other world any time he liked. Or was it only possible when he was scared out of his wits? At any rate, the fact of the matter stood – Jim was scared but when he travelled to this other world, he was no longer scared. Unnerved a little by being on a merchant ship and in the midst of a battle? Yes. But scared? No! Jim spent more time daydreaming at the possibilities of this world than he did eating his dinner, and his brother just stared at him from the other side of the table. John looked at Jim as if he were someone he didn't recognize and he was trying to figure out why. It was a funny situation. Jim was trying to grasp what had just happened to him, and John was doing the very same thing.

"Well, his clothes are all dry now," Theresa said as she walked into the kitchen to finish eating her sandwich. "I was even able to get the smell of all that saltwater off of them."

Then she said, "I am not sure how you got all that mess on you, and, at this point, I'm not sure I even care. Here's the deal. If you won't tell mom we left you alone, we won't tell her about your little water seaweed mess. Deal?"

Jim, still in a daze, simply nodded his head, as if he knew exactly what she was talking about, but that didn't matter to Theresa; she took it as a deal. John was still quiet. He just sat and staring at Jim like a strange insect under a glass.

Theresa stood against the counter eating the last bites of her sandwich with focused concentration. John turned to her and said, "You know we're lucky that nothing happened to him, don't ya?"

Theresa froze in mid-chew, and just nodded her head, knowing now that they made a stupid decision to leave their little brother alone just to go visit some friends down the street for a few hours. It was a decision that they would remember for years to come.

They tiredly cleaned the kitchen, and began getting ready for bed. The stress of bad decisions, and strange realities wiped out any desire to stay up later. Theresa made sure that Jim was tucked into bed after Theresa read him a story and said prayers with him, and John made sure the house was locked up like his mom showed him how to do. Then they turned out the lights, and went to bed.

Normally they all fell asleep rather quickly. Tonight, however, they all lay in bed trying to figure out all what took place today. Despite their exhaustion, their minds were racing a mile a minute. John and Theresa were just grateful that nothing worse happened to Jim. Jim was just grateful to be back home with his brother and sister.

During the night, Jim's mother came home from work, and she could not help but check in on her little chicks as they slept. She saw that John and Theresa were sleeping soundly in their beds, and then she came to Jim's room. She walked up next to his bed, and gently touched his face and hair as he held his teddy bear tightly. She smiled at him, and then turned to leave the room. As she stealthily closed the door and put herself to bed, she was grateful she could rely on her two oldest to take care of her baby boy.

Chapter 2 - Devastating News

For several years Jim and his family stayed in Delevan, because his mom had a good job and they had plenty of support from their extended family. Four years went by and towards the end of that time his mother met another man, Brent Borgins. Brent was someone who went to school with Anel growing up, but moved to Waukegan, Illinois when his dad's job transferred him there. It was not a drastic move, though, since Waukegan was only about an hour away. It had been a year since Brent's wife died and it was almost four years since Lawrence passed away.

Brent went up to Delavan to visit some old friends and to attend a family reunion. While he was there, he ran into Anel one day at the local grocery store, and they ended up getting coffee together. They talked for several hours until Anel realized that she needed to get home before the kids got back from school. They exchanged contact information, and decided to stay in touch. Both of them felt that they found someone in whom they could confide.

From that point on, Brent and Anel corresponded through letters, talked over the phone as much as possible, and Brent began making excuses to travel to Delavan on the weekends. Anel knew her relationship with Brent was getting more and more serious, but she was not quite sure how (or when) she wanted to talk to the children about him. She decided the best thing was to invite Brent over to Bill and Nora's farm when she took the kids over there on a Saturday. That way it would not be so awkward for the children to meet him, and it would give her family time to meet Brent as well. The farm seemed to be the best neutral ground.

For the most part, the plan succeeded. Anel's family took to Brent right away. It helped that Bill knew Brent from years past, but they were never close friends. John and Theresa took to Brent very well. Theresa did, especially, because she knew that her mom was lonely, and she came to terms, as best she could, with the fact that her mother could one day have a new husband. John was somewhat indifferent; neither resistant nor fully willing to embrace Brent. Jim had the hardest time.

He simply did not understand who this man was, and why he was invited to their weekly family outing to Uncle Bill's farm. The thing that he found hardest to comprehend, though, was why was this man was holding his mother's hand?! His dad always held his mother's hand when they were out and about, and now *this* guy was holding his mother's hand.

Jim stayed away most of the time they were at Bill and Nora's. He was either playing in the barn, messing with the cows or he was out walking in the fields. He thought much about his time on the warship and the battle against Captain Fobos. The memories from that journey were still so fresh and vivid. It was over three years since that time, and Jim wondered if he would ever face another situation that would cause him to go within. He only came back to the house when it was time to eat and as soon as he could, he was right back in the fields. Brent and Anel were prepared for this, because they both knew that the first meeting would not be an easy meeting. It was going as well as could be expected under the circumstances.

After they all ate dinner, the guys spent some time playing horseshoes, while the ladies were engaged in a lively game of *Scrabble*. The sun would not set until late this evening, so it made for a perfect ending to a great time at the farm. They all said their goodbyes, and parted ways for the evening.

The next day Brent joined Anel and the kids at church. After the service, Brent came to their house for lunch, and Anel made spaghetti and meatballs for everyone. She even made a large, fresh loaf of French bread with a wonderful garlic butter spread in the middle. The house smelled of an authentic Italian banquet!

Theresa gave Brent a tour of the house, and John gave him a tour of the outside. Then they spent some time throwing a football around. Jim closed himself off in his room, watching out the window as Brent and John threw the football around. He could smell the food cooking, and was getting so hungry by now. No matter how hungry he was, though, he was not willing to budge an inch with this guy, this intruder!

Jim determined that this man would not replace his dad, so, like China and its Great Wall, he threw up all his defenses. And he would keep them erected as long as it took, as far as he was concerned. For now, though, it was time to eat, and, no matter how defensive he was, he was not going to miss his mom's cooking.

The air was thick around the dinner table. To add insult to injury, Jim had to sit right next to Brent, but he refused to hold his hand while they said grace. As soon as he finished gobbling down dinner, he asked to be excused from the table, and back up to his room he went.

Jim watched through the window as Brent was about to leave. That is when he saw the unpardonable: he saw Brent kiss his mother on the cheek before they parted! First he holds her hand, and now he kissed his mother. What next? Would he ask her to marry him?! He could hardly stomach the thought.

The next week Brent came up again, and they all met at Bill and Nora's farm. However, Anel and Brent went out on a date by themselves, leaving the kids at the farm. Jim did not like this at all, and he knew that nothing good could come of this. They were gone for what seemed like ages, and it was getting close to being dark already.

Everyone was now inside the house either playing a board game together or reading a book or the newspaper. It was a little past eight o'clock when some car headlights beamed through the living room window. Jim watched through the window as his mother and Brent got out of the car, and came toward the house. They seemed to be acting very bubbly together, and Jim knew something fishy was going on.

Nora let the two inside, and both of them were grinning from ear to ear like a couple of kids in a candy store. That is when the words burst out of Anel's mouth, "We're engaged!" as she showed off the ring to everyone. The whole house erupted into an uproar, and there were hugs and handshakes all around. Jim, however, was mortified.

When everyone quieted down for a moment, Anel shared something else, "We are getting married at the end of the month, so the kids can finish school. We are heading to Hawaii for our honeymoon, and when we get back, we are all moving to Waukegan, to move into Brent's house!"

Bill and Nora were still very excited for Anel and Brent, but none of the cousins were very excited by this additional news. Jim was absolutely livid! He gritted his teeth as he felt his face getting hot from anger. He burst out the back door, and up into the hayloft he climbed.

He felt overwhelmed with a feeling of betrayal. Jim believed that his mother committed the unforgivable sin by agreeing to marry another man. *"How could she? She is so mean! Why would she do this? Who is this guy anyways?"* Like a hive of bees all as busy as can be, these were the thoughts that were racing through his mind at the moment. Then his mind began to take another route, *"Did she say that we are moving to Illinois after they get married?"*

That meant they would be moving away from Uncle Bill and Aunt Nora, away from his cousins, away from Grandpa and Grandma, away from his friends at school. It meant they would have to completely start over as a family, and they had to do so with this strange man. This last mental trail seemed to be absolutely unbearable. Jim collapsed on a bale of hay, and pulled his knees to his chest as he sat against the barn wall.

He was so angry at his mother, but more than that, he became very afraid of what lay ahead. The more he thought about leaving Delavan and moving to Waukegan and the more he thought about leaving everything that he ever knew, to start a whole new life, the more the weight of fear began to crush his soul.

Jim sat staring into the dark cool air within the barn, and tears began to stream down his cheeks. His mind wandered through his imagination. As he peered straight ahead, it seemed as if the very air in the barn began to pulse, like an octopus traversing the ocean. The pulses became larger and larger and stronger and stronger until...

Chapter 3 - The Jungle Calls

All of a sudden the dark pulses stopped and the quiet night became deathly silent. The smell of the barn with hay and animals was no longer present. The aroma of flowers and trees overwhelmed the nostrils, as well as the pungent smell of sweat and body odor. The air was no longer cool and clammy, typical of those Wisconsin spring nights. Instead it was rather humid and stuffy. Jim had not experienced such a warm night but as he stared into the dark, he felt the difference on his skin and in the air he breathed.

He realized that he was no longer sitting down, but now lay on his back, swaying ever so slightly back and forth in what seemed like some hanging net. He was actually lying in a hammock for the first time in his life. His skin felt awkward as well, because he was used to the sensation of having a shirt, pants, and shoes on when he was outside. As he began to feel for his shirt and pants, that is when he realized that he was not dressed at all, but only had on some type of hard stone or bone necklace, which was sitting on his chest, and a leather wrap that felt similar to shorts. It was so dark that he could not really tell.

Curiosity started to take hold of Jim's mind, because he began to realize that he was no longer in Delavan: he had once again journeyed to another world! He had longed to again experience another alternate reality for years, and now he was here. That is when the questions began to pour into his nine-year-old mind: *Where am I? Who am I with? Am I still with Captain Dojure and did we make it to the island at last? If so, is Captain Fobos still after us?* These thoughts flooded his mind at the moment, and he began to feel unsettled. He had to know.

Jim lifted his head up a little from the hammock to take a look around. It was not as dark as he previously thought, because the flickering light of what appeared to be a fire was peeking in through several cracks of whatever place he was in. It provided enough light for Jim to realize that he was not alone. This was some type of hut, and there were close to twenty other people (men, women, and children) lying in the same type of "bed" he had. This threw his mind for a loop for sure, because there were no women and children on board the warship in his last excursion. *"Who are these people?"* Jim wondered.

He was full of curiosity, but thought it best to investigate when morning came. He hoped that it would be soon, because his stomach was growling as much as his mind was curious! Jim lay back down and closed his eyes hoping to fall asleep quickly. Surprisingly he did, and in the morning he awoke to the sound of low-toned voices outside of the bungalow.

As he opened his eyes, he faintly caught the image of some creature above his head, and as quick as a cat rolled to his left, falling several feet to the dirt floor. He quickly shot to his feet to see what the creature was, but by that time all he could see was its tail, as it darted through a small hole in the wall. He was the only person left in the sleeping area.

His stomach prodded him to go outside, because it desired to be filled. He cautiously walked to the doorway of the hut, and as he crossed the threshold, he scanned from left to right. His hut was not the *only* one: this was an entire village. There were about ten huts that he could count, and outside of each one there was a fire with a gaggle of people gathered around. It appeared that he was not the only hungry person.

From the doorway he noticed that even though this was a village of some sort, there was something different about his hut. His hut seemed to be separated from the other huts. The separation was not great, by any means, but it was certainly noticeable right away. This definitely piqued Jim's interest, but he had to address that question later. At the moment, he had his stomach to attend to before it launched a mutiny against him.

He left the doorway of the bungalow, and meandered up to the crowd of people around the fire. It felt strange because once again he was keenly aware that he was not at home. And even though he knew this, he felt very much at peace with his new surroundings. It was such a strange phenomenon, yet, no matter how strange it was, it was somehow comforting.

As he sat down near the fire, he noticed that he was not the only person there with few clothes on. Everyone was dressed very minimally, including himself. This was odd because you were usually fully dressed in Wisconsin, especially in the winters. But the weather here was rather warm and definitely humid. Jim had sweat on his forehead already and it was only sunrise. Jim thought, "If it's this hot in the morning, then what is it gonna be like in the afternoon?"

All of a sudden, a boy walked over to him and handed him some meat from whatever animal they were roasting over the fire. Jim was not sure what this would taste like, but he was too hungry to debate with himself about whether to eat it or not. He nibbled it to try it out and to his astonishment, it tasted just like chicken! "Oh thank God," he said to himself. He gobbled down the rest of the meat. A woman passed a bowl to him that had some type of paste in it that looked like a variety of fruit. It was a red and orange mixture, and the others were simply using their fingers to scoop it out and eat it. Jim followed suit. "Wow, that is really good," he thought, as he devoured the entire bowl.

He saw a couple of people go to a large bucket, and scoop out something to drink. He hoped it was water, so he stood up and went over to the bucket. Sure enough it was. He bent over and drank almost too much water. He was very thirsty, and this heat did not help at all.

When he was finished drinking, he went back to the same spot by the fire, and just watched everyone else. Most people were just staring into the flames, while seeming to mindlessly do something with their hands: either make arrows or braid a basket or the like. A couple of small children were already running around trying to catch bugs and one another. Jim observed that it seemed to be like this around the entire village.

Nobody was really talking yet. An occasional nod or whistle to get someone's attention, but that was about it. There were no coffee pots for sure, something he was used to seeing his mom partake of each morning, as most adults did in his world. So maybe this was the next best thing: a fire and some meat with a little fruit paste. Oh well, Jim did not mind, because either way he was able to quell his rebellious stomach for now.

After about an hour or so of this scenario, the men began to separate from the women and children, and that is when one of the men called to Jim, "Come on, let's go! We are heading out with your uncle."

"My uncle?" Jim thought. "If this guy is supposed to be my uncle, then where are my parents?" he further wondered. Nevertheless, he followed the man to where it seemed like all the men of the entire village were gathered.

The atmosphere surrounding this group of men was very tense. All of the men (and boys his age or older) were holding spears in their hands, and they all were encircled around one man. "Is this my uncle?" Jim wondered. As Jim was thinking about this, the man who brought him to the circle handed him his own spear. Jim wasn't sure if he wanted to take it, because he was uncertain as to why everyone was holding one.

As he was admiring the spear in his hand, the man in the middle began to speak. "You know why we have all gathered here this morning," he said. "Today is the day my nephew is to make his Great Hunt," he continued, and at that moment everyone turned towards Jim as they all let out a collective, "Beeeelllllooooo!"

Jim was dumbstruck and did not know what to do. But the circle opened up as hands everywhere seemed to push him into the middle.

Pulling Jim close to his side with his arm around his shoulder, his uncle spoke up once again, "Today, as we hunt for our families, my nephew Bjime will lead us to the den of the horned boar, and he will kill his first beast! We all know that his father very much looked forward to this day. We also know that one day soon we will avenge his father and mother's death," his uncle said.

At this, the group yelled an even louder, "Beeeeeellllllllooooooooo," as they all thrust their spears into the air, startling Jim to his core!

After this, as if on cue, they all broke the circle and gathered into groups. Jim just followed his uncle and as he did, a young man came up to his uncle, "Turlow, we have found fresh boar tracks to the south."

Turlow responded, "Then let us be on our way."

Now Jim, if he knew nothing else about his present situation, at least he now knew his uncle's name.

As they walked into the jungle, Jim looked back toward the village huts, and he noticed that all of the women and little children watched as the men vanished into the tree line. They had a look on their faces that said, "We hope they bring some very good meat back!" Jim just simply did not want to die.

"How can I lead a hunt? Jim questioned himself. "I don't know a cotton-pickin' thing about hunting an animal, let alone hunting one with a dumb spear!" Whether he knew how to hunt (with a spear or anything else), the fact of the matter was that he was going on a hunt, and to top it all off, he had to lead it.

Turlow walked very close to Jim, so this put him at ease a bit. This reminded him of his time with Captain Dojure, and it took his mind back to that old merchant ship for a few moments. Once they entered the jungle, there were so many paths to choose from that Jim had not a clue where to go. Thankfully, the young man who sighted the fresh boar tracks earlier was apparently the *de facto* guide for the group, which lifted a load of worry from Jim. He said to himself, "I just need to follow this guide, and stick close to Turlow. And when this beast comes out, I will just try and aim for its side." He figured that was his best chance, since the side of the beast had more striking area. Jim tried to reassure himself but he was not doing a very good job at it. Oh well. The trek continued.

They walked for hours it seemed. Jim was very thirsty by now, and thankfully they crossed over a couple of streams. He noticed that others were stopping by these streams to snag a drink with their hands, so at the next stream Jim did so himself. He could tell that it was nearing mid-day, because the sun was directly over their heads, which did not help at all. Even though the jungle was very dense, some of the sun's rays could still be slightly seen. It was definitely hotter now, but Jim was thankful that the foliage from the dense tropical jungle provided some much needed shade as they walked along.

There were probably over forty men and boys in this group and as they travelled along, they would sometimes spread out along parallel paths. When it was a narrower area they all fell back in line on the guide's path. Turlow yelled up to the guide, "Pishta, what do you see?"

Pishta yelled back over his shoulder, "We are close."

Jim now knew the guide's name, so he just needed to remember it.

"Bjime, when we reach the boar's den, do not be afraid. We are all here to help you," Turlow said. "I was afraid when it was time for me to go on my Great Hunt as well. Did you know that your father and I went on our Great Hunt together?"

Jim just shook his head . As Turlow continued to speak to him, Jim discovered that his uncle and his father in this tribe were twin brothers, but his father had been born first. Thus, he was the tribe's chief until his untimely death.

At that moment, his mind travelled back to Delavan, back to his normal reality, and he could picture everyone sitting in Uncle Bill's house. He wondered what his family was doing while he was leading this boar hunt. Whatever they were doing, he did not care, because he was still furiously mad at his mother. His mind came back to the jungle, and he noticed that everyone began to walk more stealthily. There was no more joking or cackling between people, but only the sound of anxious thoughts piercing through the thick jungle air could be heard.

As the trail descended into a lower area of the jungle, Jim knew that they must be nearing the boar's cave, because he himself saw large split-hoof tracks some ways back. They looked reminiscent of the tracks that the pigs on his uncle's farm made, but these tracks were nearly four times the size! This unnerved Jim to say the least. There was no turning back at this point, and in a short while, either Jim would be killed or this boar would be.

You see, Jim (or Bjime as his fellow tribesmen called him) was now walking with the Chewalah tribe, and the premiere rite of passage into manhood for any boy was to kill a boar. But for those who were of the royal line, they were expected to kill a *horned* boar, which were almost three times the size of a normal boar.

Bjime's father and mother were the Chiefs of the Chewalah tribe, and their enemies from the Wagura tribe assassinated them one night by releasing poisonous snakes into their bungalow. The Chewalah tribe had invited the Wagura tribe to a feast to promote peace between the two tribes, and during the feast the Chief of the Wagura tribe, Fobosu, was to betroth his daughter, Ankara, to the son of the Chief of the Chewalah's. That happened to be Bjime.

However, before the betrothal could take place, Fobosu and his men killed the Chief of the Chewalahs along with his wife, and they snuck away into the jungle during the night. In the morning, the Chewalahs realized what had happened but by that time, there was nothing they could do. The entire tribe was utterly devastated.

The hunt for the horned boar was to be initiated by the father of the royal son, and it was to symbolize the preparation of the son to be the next heir of the tribe. But since Bjime's father had been killed, the king's twin brother, Turlow, was now the acting king until Bjime reached the age of inheritance. Needless to say, this hunt was bittersweet for the Chewalah tribe, because they were celebrating the inauguration of the future king while still mourning the death of the former.

The chiefs' deaths only took place several weeks before, so the anger of the Chewalahs was still white hot. They were simply waiting for the prime moment for which they could exact their revenge. They waited for the dark quarter of the moon and then they would strike!

Bjime was completely unaware of this entire situation between the two tribes, and I am sure that, if he did know, the fright of spearing this infamous horned boar would certainly be eclipsed by sharing their anger in his parents' deaths. Beyond killing this boar, a devastating war between the Chewalahs and the Waguras loomed on the horizon! But for now, Bjime must survive this hunt.

The group of men now fanned out as the royal party continued straight down the path toward the boar's cave. Bjime noticed that a type of arena was naturally formed into the jungle, and it seemed that the boar happened to live within it. There was no speaking at all by this time, only hand gestures and subtle whistling for communication. They knew that the horned boar was a fierce beast and if it was startled before they were set to kill it, it could mean the death for some in their tribe.

Pishta continued to guide the royal party down the path, and having him lead right now brought a sense of comfort to Jim. At that moment, he looked up to his right and left around the jungled-arena and noticed that the rest of the men were stealthily surrounding it. Jim noticed that some of the men were not present, but at the time he did not think anything of it. His mind was completely preoccupied. He thought to himself, "What sort of fierce beast is this that the entire male population of this village finds it necessary to surround it?" That question would soon be answered.

Before they entered the open area of the arena, Turlow stopped Bjime and spoke to him very softly, "Remember that your father is with you right now. Remember that he is proud of you, and that so am I. But also remember that if you do not kill the horned boar, your right to the throne of the Chewalah people will go to my son. So kill well, my nephew. For you and your family!"

As Turlow spoke to him, Bjime thought to himself, "Is this supposed to encourage me?"

As they entered the arena, he noticed the stone walls went up thirty feet all around, and tapered down towards their path. There was one way in and one way out. Pishta was no longer at the point, but took his place towards the rear. It was now Bjime's turn to lead the royal party into the dreaded abode of the horned boar.

Bjime took the point and as he slowly crept forward, the royal party fanned out along the tree line of the arena. Bjime did not know if this was them saying, "We are here to help, if it comes to that," or "You kill that boar or you will not make it out of here alive." The whole situation left him terrified, his breath coming in pants. Part of him wished he was back in Wisconsin at the moment, but he still was still furiously angry with his mother.

He slowly inched forward, tightly gripping his spear, and sweat poured down his forehead like a miserable drizzle of rain. He tried his best to wipe the sweat with his forearms while holding the spear with a death grip with his hands, but that just seemed to smear the sweat at best. And now, some of the sweat funneled into his right eye. "I'm in a strange place, with some weird people, wearing almost no clothing, hunting some leviathan of a beast, and now I can only see out of my left eye. Just great!" Jim grumbled under his breath.

No matter how disconcerting the situation was, Bjime was now determined to kill this oversized pig! At that moment, all the anger towards his mother along with the impatience of his heightened anxiety drove him to act. With these emotions a rush of courage came over him and he stood up straight and walked more stoutly. As he neared the entrance of the cave, he bent over to pick up a couple of stones, and he began to throw them into the mouth of the cave, while yelling loudly to stir up the boar.

After a few moments, Bjime could hear something stirring from within the cave, so he braced himself. He was ready at any moment to thrust his spear through this animal, and he stood poised to do just that. The guttural noise from the cave grew louder and louder, and it seemed to be coming faster and faster. In a flash, the beast crossed the threshold of the cave, and bolted straight toward him.

In a split second, he was caught off guard, and started to step backwards. As he did, he tripped on a rock and as he fell, he could see the boar rushing at him. Jim had no other choice but to the thrust his spear as hard as he could at it. Without any assurance that he was throwing it in the correct direction, he released his spear as hard as he humanly could.

He fell back hard, and slammed his right elbow on a rock. Then, as quick as a mongoose, he was on his feet again. But something was awry! The "beast" just stood there staring at him. All of the sudden, all of the men surrounding the arena erupted in screaming laughter. There, standing before Bjime was a beast alright. It was a giant costume with about ten men underneath it, and by this time they came out from beneath it. They too, were now joining in the festive laughter, and all of the men were rushing down to the entrance of the arena and towards Bjime.

Apparently this was a rite of passage for the heir, but it had nothing to do with whether or not he became the next chief. It was a gargantuan practical joke the entire village played on the king's son before it was his time to become the new ruler. Usually, the chief himself was the maestro of the event but since Bjime's father was murdered, Turlow took the reins. Luckily, Bjime's father was planning this joke for some time, so Turlow already knew the entire plan. And so did everyone else.

By now, they gathered around Bjime, and helped him to his feet as they laughed and laughed and laughed. They kept patting him on his back, reassuring him that he had performed superbly. They also let him know that they saw nothing more funny in their lives. Bjime was utterly stunned to say the least, and kept circling and touching the "beast." He could not fathom how realistic this costume looked, and wondered what would have happened, if this was a real animal. As he circled back around to the front of the animal, he got his answer. For there, he saw that his spear penetrated the breast of the beast right below its neck line. Thankfully for the perpetrators of the joke, they reinforced the boar costume with some very strong tree bark, so that the spear would not harm anyone.

Now began the long trek back to the village, and all along the way the men joked with one another. Bjime was relieved to know that he did not have to actually kill some raging beast, but now he felt like the village boob for sure. At least he was still alive.

As they neared the village, the sound of the children playing and the women gathering could be heard through the trees of the forest. The smell of meat cooking filled Bjime's nostrils, and this triggered his stomach, the one beast that truly did exist.

When they cleared the threshold of the tree line and entered the village, there was laughter and clapping all around, and the Chewalahs were very jubilant. They all gathered in the main assembly area and to Bjime's astonishment, what was roasting on the fire for dinner? You guessed it: boar!

Apparently the entire village was in on this ruse. But the playful atmosphere would not last long because tomorrow night was the dark quarter of the moon, and the Chewalahs were poised to exact their vengeance on Waguras. For tonight, any thoughts of vengeance were placed aside to celebrate with the eating of freshly roasted boar meat.

Turlow stood at the front of the assembled village, and called Bjime to himself. "Brothers and sisters. My fellow Chewalahs. Today was a day of joking and celebration, as is the custom before the new chief takes his place among us. Everyone involved performed wonderfully, and truly the events at the cave today were everything we could have hoped for. We hoped for laughter, and that is what we reaped." Turlow continued, "But we also received something else unexpectedly, something far greater. Bravery! Today, we saw the bravery and cunning of our future ruler, our future chief, and had that gargantuan creature been real it would have most certainly been slain. For our very own Bjime thrust his spear through its breast below its neck, and no beast, whatever it be, would have withstood the force of his attack. We are truly fortunate to have such a brave and fierce warrior as our soon to be chief."

"Bellllllloooooooo," cheered the entire village.

Bjime felt completely embarrassed, and he could feel himself turning red. He wished he was a bird at the moment, so he could fly away. But his wings failed to sprout.

Turlow began speaking again, "Tonight, as we celebrate our future chief, let us also remember our former. Let us remember Bjime's father and mother. For soon we will take our revenge!"

"Beeellllloooooooo!" cried everyone together. And with that, the celebration for the night commenced. There was dancing and games and food and drinks all around. Children were running and playing every which way while the elders of the village sat still near the fire peacefully taking in the celebration.

It was a wonderful scene to behold because though these were the most rudimentary of people, they could not have been more exuberant. They had life, food, one another, and nothing more could make them more grateful. Bjime was enthralled in the midst of this happiness, and he took it all in. Certainly nobody in Wisconsin would have celebrated with as much enthusiasm as these people were doing. He did not care and jumped in the dancing and the games, and he ate all the boar that he could stand (which tasted much like the pigs from his uncle's farm). As far as he could tell for the moment, he was a Chewalah.

Despite all the festivities, Bjime could not get the words of Turlow out of his mind, "Let us remember Bjime's father and mother. For soon we will take our revenge!"

"What did he mean by this?" Bjime wondered to himself. That nagging question tried to dampen the exuberant spirit of the night within him, but he held it at bay. He would find out the answer to his question later.

After several hours, the fires died down and the people slowly returned to their bungalows. Bjime looked up towards the heavens, and noticed how brilliantly the stars shown against the dark night sky. He remembered sitting in the pew of his church on a Sunday listening to his pastor speak of how God created each one of those stars. This thought enraptured his mind and soul, and he took much comfort from it. It was a long day, though, and he was completely exhausted from all the day's events. He returned to his family's bungalow, and he crawled up to his hammock some six feet off the ground. Not bad for his first day as a Chewalah.

He slept as soundly as could be expected. As Jim slept, he dreamt of his family back in Wisconsin. He could see everyone inside in Bill and Nora's house, and he could see them all celebrating over his mother and Brent's engagement. He could also see himself in Bill's barn with his back against the wall, knees drawn up, sitting on a bale of hay, and he could literally feel the anger that exuded from within his own soul. This anger left him with an uneasy feeling as he lay dreaming in his hammock, and the aftertaste was even worse when he awoke in the morning.

As the sun rose, the jungle's soul rose with it. The birds and monkeys seemed to be different parts of a natural chorus, sent by their creator to rouse their human counterparts from sweet slumber. The plan apparently worked perfectly, because as the animals began their beautifully crafted song the villagers began to awaken. They began coming out of their bungalows to stoke their fires, and began the morning chores of gathering water, food, and wood for the fires. Children were usually some of the first ones awake, and their innocent voices would intertwine with the jungle song of the morning, making one pleasant melody in which to wake up. This song plus the fact that it does not take long for the bungalows to heat up in the mornings forced people outside, unless it was pouring down rain.

Jim crawled down from his hammock, and slowly walked outside. He could not believe that he was still with the Chewalahs. He thought he would be back in Wisconsin by now, because his inaugural journey to a different realm lasted only half a day or so. He had been in the jungle about a full day. This did not worry him necessarily, but it was definitely something of which he took note.

As he stepped out of his bungalow, although the morning glories abounded around him, he could feel that this day was different, much different than the one previous. The first difference he noticed was that every adult that was awake was primarily sitting around either sharpening spears or arrows. This was a daunting sight for certain. The distinct smell of battle floated in the air.

Jim was taking in the scene and was not exactly sure what to make of everything before his eyes. He knew the inevitable outcome to all the effort everyone was putting forth would be a major battle between these two jungle tribes. And he wondered if he would again be part of another battle, or would he be back in Wisconsin before then. Whatever the outcome, he needed to quell the battle within his stomach at the moment!

Making his way toward the water pot he took a few sips of water to wet his lips. As he bent over to get some water, he saw the reflection of his face for the first time. He startled and jumped back. Jim noticed that in this world he was a few years older. His face looked somewhat more mature, and it was pronouncedly thinner than the chubby Wisconsin-cheesed face he was used to seeing in the mirror each day. He looked like a teenager. "How weird," Jim thought, as he felt his face with both hands.

As he stared at his reflection in the water bucket, the same boy, Pishta, who had brought him food the morning before brought Jim some meat to munch on, which made his stomach most delighted. Jim found the bowl of fruit paste to go with the mystery meat, and before long he had eaten enough to stave off his hunger.

As he was eating, he noticed that his right elbow was in excruciating pain from yesterday's hunt, when he tripped and slammed his elbow on a rock. Hopefully he did not break anything. And hopefully it would not be hurting when he returned, *if he returned*, to Wisconsin. This trip was already turning out to be more than he bargained for.

The sun started to crest over the tree line by now and the temperature steadily rose. Jim did his best to help out where needed, but he was not exactly sure what to do. As he sat making some arrows, he noticed his Uncle Turlow was having a heated argument with one of the other tribesman. They were on the outskirts of the village with several of the other men around listening intently to this exchange.

At one point, the other man stormed off angrily towards his bungalow, and sat down near the fire as he obviously stewed. Turlow was equally, visibly angry, and he came huffing and puffing back towards Jim's bungalow. He walked past Jim and disappeared into the forest, presumably to walk off his anger.

Jim turned to Pishta and asked him, "What was that all about?"

"Golu does not want us to fight the Waguras. He has family there," Pishta replied. "Golu's two sisters married into their tribe several years ago because his father owed a debt to one of the men in the Wagura tribe."

The rest of the day Jim continued helping to make arrows for the battle, and then at some point late in the afternoon, it seemed like everyone vanished all at once. Everyone retreated to their bungalows to rest. Jim assumed they were getting some sleep before the long night, so he thought it would be best to follow suit. He crawled back up the six feet to his hammock and dozed off.

When he awoke no one was in the bungalow. He was late to nap time and late to wake up. Hopefully this was not an omen concerning how the night was going to go. As he stepped out of the bungalow, he noticed the sun starting to set, and a full, bright moon was already rising in its place.

Jim was somewhat stunned at what he saw next. All of the male members of the tribe were having paint applied to their faces and bodies and Jim could only guess that this was war paint. "What is it with going to war and paint," Jim thought to himself? He had not walked twenty feet before some of the women began using him as a human canvas. He jokingly said out loud, "So this is what it must have felt like to be the Sistine Chapel." The women just gave him an odd look and kept on applying the paint.

After what seemed like forever (twenty minutes), the women moved onto another unsuspecting male, and Jim drew near Pishta. He noticed that Turlow was back from the forest and that he was already well painted. Like a good general, he was going around to the different bungalows to check on all the men. When he saw that Jim was all painted, he made his way over.

Turlow walked up to Jim and said, "You look very fine, Bjime. I would be very afraid of you, if I were your enemy! You will make a great warrior tonight as we take vengeance on the Waguras for what they did to your parents, to my brother and his wife. Just remember that your father and mother will be with you in this battle, and they will help give you strength and protect you. Just use that spear as mighty as you did against the boar yesterday, and you will strike down our foes." He patted Jim on the shoulders and moved on.

Jim thought to himself, "And this is supposed to encourage me? At what point do I make it back to Wisconsin? If I was gone for only two hours last time which turned out to be a half a day, since I have been gone for almost two days now, how long have I been gone from Wisconsin?" This last thought brought a great deal of disconcertment, because he knew that his family, especially his mother, would be terribly worried for him.

It was now dark. Nobody ate dinner and Jim noticed that he was not even hungry. Nervous? Yes! The men were all passing around this foul tasting drink. Nobody guzzled it, but all the men were certainly partaking. When it was Jim's turn, he briefly sniffed it before taking some into his mouth. That probably was not the best idea, because it only exacerbated the situation, since the drink tasted far worse than it smelled. He just managed to gulp it down and pass it to the man on his left.

There was a full moon this night. This would provide the necessary light the Chewalahs needed to ambush the Waguras. After the foul drink made its round to all the men, they all gathered near Turlow's bungalow, all armed and painted for battle. Turlow explained the battle plan to the men. They would break into three parties, and surround the Wagura village. Turlow said that when his party shot a fire arrow into the air all parties were to converge on the seemingly unsuspecting tribe. But he gave orders that none of the women or children were to be killed in this raid, if it could be helped.

He warned all the men to be leery of Fobosu. "Fobosu is very crafty, and he will show you no mercy. So give him none yourself!" He continued, "Remember how he assassinated our chief and his wife in their sleep, while staying in our camp under a banner of peace. And now let his cunning return on his own head!"

All the men resoundingly cheered, "Beeeeeelllllllllllooooo!!!" Turlow raised his spear in the air, and all the men chanted loudly, "Bello, Bello, Bello!"

Jim was not sure how to feel at that moment. He knew that in reality he was simply a young boy from Wisconsin, who was at that very moment crying on a pile of hay in his uncle's barn. This he knew for sure. How to fight an enemy in the midst of a jungle with a spear by the light of the moon? This he had no clue about. But there was no backing out at that point.

Turlow began to break the men up into their respective parties and as he did so, he noticed that Golu was not present.

"Where is Golu?" Turlow yelled. "Where is he?" he repeated.

Pishta ran to his bungalow and others checked around the village, but he was nowhere to be found. Everyone knew what this meant; he had betrayed their tribe. Turlow ordered his wife and children to be kept under guard until after the battle, so Golu's wife was tied up and she and her children were thrown into a storage bungalow and secured shut.

Golu must have gone to warn the Waguras, and the Waguras would be waiting for them, if Golu got there before them. There was no time to lose. Time was now of the essence. Turlow quickly broke the tribe into three parties, and Jim was placed in Turlow's party. As soon as the parties were separated, they set off for the Wagura's village at breakneck speed. Normally it would take three or four hours to make the trek to their village, but at this speed they would be there in two hours.

Even though they were moving at the pace of a deer through well-worn jungle paths, as they ran along, memories of running through the forest in Wisconsin seemed to intermingle with the current reality before him. It was a strange feeling, because it was as if the two worlds were as one at that moment. The mind is certainly a fascinating creation, and capable of such great imaginary and creative power. Jim was getting but a taste of the outer limits of its scope.

The Chewalahs sped along like panthers in their element, but not one sound escaped their mouths. They were very disciplined, because they knew that they needed to preserve what little element of surprise they had left, no thanks to Golu. Somehow Jim felt this was just another battle for him, as if he had already been in dozens of them. In reality, this was the furthest thing from the truth. He began to mentally prepare for how he would react, once they confronted the opposing tribe. Despite the fact that his right elbow was still in great pain, he tried to envision himself attacking them just as he did against the horned-boar. This provided a sense of calm upon which his emotions could latch. That, and the fact that his Uncle Turlow would be close by in this battle, just as Captain Dojure was in his first excursion within.

After about an hour of running at such a great speed, they stopped at a brook to refresh themselves before making the last leg of their journey. Jim observed the moon during this short respite, and he noticed how wonderfully bright it was. He took note of the craters that seemed much more pronounced on that night. Maybe it was the adrenaline flowing through his veins that sharpened his vision, or maybe it was just the sheer brilliance of the dark, jungle night sky. Either way, it was a captivatingly peaceful moment in the midst of such impending destruction.

Turlow spoke softly, "Let's go. Keep quiet. If you see something suspicious, whistle to alert everyone." And just as suddenly as they had stopped they were back at panther speed, moving mightily yet stealthily upon the moonlit jungle path.

After about another hour at this speed, they slowed their pace to a brisk walk. They were now off the main path and were spread out to avoid an ambush. The party crept quietly to the edge of the forest where the village clearing began. Everyone was crouched down, awaiting directions from Turlow. Something was not right. It was quiet, but it all seemed too quiet.

Turlow decided to send scouts in sets of two out around the perimeter of the village to assess if the other parties were in place. After twenty minutes, the set of scouts that went out to the west came back and reported that the other party was indeed there and in place. However, the scouts that took off to the east still had not returned. This was a bad omen for sure. Turlow decided to confide in one of his other leaders. They began weighing their options.

If they proceeded with the current plan, they could be walking into an uncertain trap, and many, if not all the men could lose their lives. But if they did not proceed they would lose any element of surprise they may still have, and miss the opportunity to strike the Waguras by the light of the moon. There was no choice left. It was all or nothing.

Turlow informed the men to ready for the attack. The bowman lit his arrow, and, in the blink of an eye, his arrow shot aloft, high above the tree line. And with that one shot the Chewalah men all rushed the Wagura village.

They rushed from one bungalow to the next, each man yelling, "Bellllooo!" at the top of his lungs. But every bungalow they searched yielded the same result: nobody was there. The entire village was abandoned! On top of this, party number three was still not there. What did this mean?

Turlow and Bishma, the leader of the second party, gathered to discuss their next course of action. Clearly the Waguras captured or attacked the third party, but where were they? That is when the frightening thought began to sink in for the whole war party. The Waguras counter-surprised them, but to what extent nobody knew. They had no time to lose. They decided to stay together, and rush back to their own camp via the river route that Bishma's party had taken.

As they rushed along, the river dampened the sound of their heavy breathing and stomping from all the running they were doing. Bishma and Turlow were at the front of the pack, and Jim was not far behind. At one point the path disappeared and everyone was forced to cross the river at a shallow area. As they trudged through the water, their pace was abruptly stalled. It was then they realized just how crafty an enemy Fobosu truly was.

Jim followed behind Turlow and as they waded through the water, the sounds of arrows began to pierce the night sky as they flew past them striking some of the Chewalahs. Turlow was hit in the right leg and immediately went down. The entire northern bank of the river was lined with Waguras, and they pounced upon the unsuspecting Chewalahs like a lion attacking a deer stuck in a thicket.

Half of the Chewalahs charged forward to try and get out of the water to be on better footing to fight while the rear half turned back to get out of the river. They tried to return fire against the Waguras while their forward comrades charged with spears. There was no turning back for Jim, so forward it was for him. At that moment, with the light of the moon striking his face, he caught a glimpse of Fobosu. He could see him leading the assault against his fellow villagers, and he was a very fierce sight to behold. Jim noticed that he could not see his face, though, because he had some type of mask over it. The moonlight exposed that clear enough.

Turlow, with half an arrow still protruding from his leg, led the fight straight towards Fobosu, and Jim admired such a display of bravery. At this, the rear ranks of the Chewalahs leaped back into the water to quickly traverse the breadth of the river. Turlow and Jim made it to the northern riverbank, as they encountered several Wagura warriors as Jim and Turlow struck them down. A fresh volley of arrows flew over Jim's head as the Chewalahs laid down cover fire for the assault.

As they charged forward, the Waguras returned fire from the tree line, and Turlow was again struck. This time he was hit in the chest, in his left breast, and the force was so great that it sent him flying back, toppling upon Jim. They both flew back until they hit the river bank, and Turlow's body crushed Jim underneath. The combination of the force of Turlow's body hitting Jim and the two of them slamming into the riverbank knocked Jim out.

"Turloooowww, Turloooowww," Jim was yelling at the top of his lungs. He could feel the weight of something heavy resting upon him, but he was not exactly sure what it was. It did not feel like a human body, and it certainly did not *smell* like one, especially one from the jungle. Jim thought to himself, "This feels like a bale of hay." He continued, "But how can this be, there are no bales of hay around here. Unless..." He pushed the mass of weight with all his might until it rolled off him, which sent a shot of pain coursing from his right elbow. He sat up, and caught the faint sight of morning sunlight shifting in through the cracks of the barn.

"I must be back in Wisconsin. This is my uncle's barn," Jim said to himself. Then he thought, "Have I been in the barn *all* night? If so, why didn't anybody come looking for me?" Jim wondered. All of these puzzling thoughts were racing through his mind. No matter the uncertainty, his stomach demanded food and his dry mouth craved water. So, he began the descent from the tall hay loft of the barn.

Once he was down, he made his way to the house, and quietly crept inside. He did not want to wake anyone up if everyone was still sleeping. He crept through the back door that led to the kitchen, and he quickly made it to the cupboard. He grabbed a glass to get a drink of water, guzzling down three cups worth in a matter of seconds. Now it was time to attend to his growling stomach. He opened the refrigerator, and was slightly bent over as he assessed the contents, when he heard a familiar soft voice behind him say, "Are you hungry?"

He froze, because he knew it was his mother. He slowly stood up, closed the refrigerator, and turned around.

As soon as he turned around, his mother jumped back and screamed, "Aaaaggghhh!" "James Frederich L'Beau, what the heck is all over your face?" she angrily questioned.

Jim was mortified, yet curious himself. "What *is* on my face?" he wondered. Then the thought hit him, "Could it be the war paint?" He ran to the bathroom to look in the mirror, and the sight shocked him as he jumped back with a scream as well. Right then, the pain in his right elbow manifested again. "Oww," Jim said out loud as he cupped his right elbow with his left hand. Then the memories of his time with the Chewalahs came flooding back.

Jim could hear his mother outside the bathroom, knocking and demanding answers, but all he could think about was Turlow and his fellow villagers. Did they win the battle? Were they slaughtered? Did they defeat Fobosu? But they would forever go unanswered, because the reality was that he was back in Wisconsin. He had survived another journey within to the other world, but now he needed to survive the mother-storm brewing outside the bathroom. He quickly began to wash the paint from his face, but then realized that the paint was still all over his body.

He told his mother, "I need to take a shower, and then I will be down for breakfast." That seemed to appease her for the moment, because she stopped knocking and demanding answers.

He was in no hurry to finish his shower, because he knew that when it was over he would have to provide some answers to his mother. "What am I going to tell her?" Jim asked himself. Jim scrubbed his body hard, because the paint was very difficult to get off. It crusted over his skin. "I'll just tell her that I snuck some paint out to the barn, and was pretending to be an Indian warrior," he said to himself. But then he wondered what he would tell her about his right elbow, because he knew he would probably need to see a doctor about it. He decided to tell her that he slipped on some hay in the barn, and whacked his elbow on the barn floor. That seemed pretty feasible.

Jim dried off from his shower, and got dressed. He slowly and sullenly made his way back to the kitchen. When he rounded the corner of the kitchen, he noticed that she had a plate of scrambled eggs and bacon with a glass of milk ready for him, while she sipped a cup of coffee. Nobody else seemed to be awake yet. For that Jim was very grateful. He slithered into his seat, and began devouring his food.

"Do you want some ketchup?" Anel asked.

Without even looking up, he simply nodded. She grabbed the ketchup from the refrigerator, and set it on the table for him. He doused his eggs with the yummy red paste, and like a powerful vacuum, he finished inhaling his food. Anel sat there patiently waiting for him to finish his food, because she wanted answers to her questions. And mama *would* have them.

As soon as Jim had only a few bites left on his plate, Anel shot a pointed look at him asking, "Do you mind telling me why your face and arms were all covered in paint this morning?"

At first, Jim dropped his head, because he felt somewhat foolish. Also, he was not comfortable with fibbing to his mother, but would she really believe him, let alone understand, if he told her the truth?

"I snuck some paint into the barn, because I wanted to pretend to be an Indian warrior," Jim said.

Anel shot back, "In the middle of the night?"

Jim swallowed his last bite of food with a large gulp, and answered, "I was angry with you last night, so I didn't care."

"Why are you angry with me, Jim?" Anel asked. She knew the reason, but she wanted him to get it off his chest.

"Because you want to replace Dad!" Jim cried.

Tears began to roll down Anel's cheeks as she replied, "Jim, nobody can ever replace your Dad, son. Please know that." She continued, "Brent will never replace your dad but if you give him a chance, I think you guys would really get along. He is very good to me, and he loves me very much. And I love him. That is why we want to get married. I know this is not easy, but can you at least try to give Brent a chance?"

Jim sat there staring at his mother. He could hear the words, but it seemed hard to comprehend them. The last question stung him, because he knew he was wrong. He knew he, at least, needed to give Brent a chance if for no other reason than for his mother's happiness. That is when, with tears coming down each cheek, he said, "I'm sorry, Mom. Yes, I can try."

That is when Anel got up from her chair, making her way around the table, and knelt down to give Jim a hug. "Jim, I love you so much, and I am so proud of the young man you are becoming," Anel lovingly said to him. Then she gently grabbed his arms and looked up into his tearful eyes, and jokingly said, "But if you ever scare me like this again, I will tan your hide!"

Jim tried to laugh with her, but winced because she was grabbing his right elbow. Anel noticed his wince, and asked him, "What's wrong?"

Jim answered, "I whacked my elbow on the barn floor last night."

Anel took a look at it and saw the large bruise. "Well, we'll have to take you to the doctor on Monday," she said.

A short while later everyone else began to stir from their dens, and they had breakfast together. Anel and the kids decided to hang out at the farm for a while, but then headed home in the afternoon. Thankfully, Anel seemed to accept everything Jim had told her, and Jim knew that was largely due to the whole wedding engagement. It turned out to be a blessing in disguise.

He was glad that she did not push him any further for answers. That afternoon they headed home, and on Monday Anel took Jim to the doctor. From the x-ray, Jim had severely bruised the bone, but thankfully nothing was broken. Jim was thankful to be alive, but this last excursion within was more than he wagered for. He faced some fears with hunting the horned-boar, trying new foods and going to battle again, but he came very close to losing his own life at the hands of Fobosu. It would be several years before Jim again travelled to another realm.

Chapter 4 - The Fog of War

Brent and Anel married that summer. They went to Hawaii for their honeymoon and were gone for over a week. While they were gone, Jim, John and Theresa stayed with Bill and Nora. When they returned, Anel and the kids sold their house in Delavan, packed up their belongings, and Brent helped them all move to Illinois into his house. The kids did not look forward to moving away from all their friends and family, but that all changed when they saw Brent's house.

He was an attorney who, despite only owning a small law practice, did very well for himself. Each of the kids had their own bedroom, so John and Theresa would no longer have to share a room. There was a dining room, a master bedroom for Anel and Brent, a large living room, and a billiards room downstairs, which John was very excited about. They also had a pool in their backyard with a slide. The kids had only ever swum in the cold Wisconsin lakes in the summer, so this would be a treat for sure. They wasted no time enjoying the amenities of their new abode.

Brent had Anel get rid of her old car and bought her a very nice, brand new Audi. German luxury cars were all the rage around Chicago at this time. She certainly had no complaints. She had agreed to become a part of Brent's church, despite some of the doctrinal differences of her former church, because she felt it was more important that their family attend church together. The blending of families is never easy.

Even though it was emotionally very difficult for the whole family to leave all their friends and family behind, Anel and the children seamlessly settled into their new life in Waukegan. Besides, they were only a hop and a skip from their old life. They could (and would) visit often. They all enjoyed the summer with swimming and sailing on Lake Michigan. Brent had a nice sail boat, and on the weekends they took time to soak up the sun and enjoy fresh air on the lake. Anel and the kids loved this dearly. And there were so many other boats on the lake they could hardly believe their eyes. They lived impoverished for so long that this new life seemed surreal. Jim knew a thing or two about surreal.

But just as all good stories must come to an end, so their summer came to an end. It was now time to face the daunting, dreadful reality known as *back-to-school*. The kids, especially John and Theresa, were not looking forward to starting at a new school, because puberty was awkward enough, without having to make all new friends. Surprisingly, Jim was somewhat ambivalent to the situation, because he was still immune to many of the social woes that being a teenager brought.

John and Theresa's bus came to pick them up around 7:30 a.m. and Jim's arrived thirty minutes later. This was the weird part for him, because he had *always* ridden the bus with his brother and sister. In their tiny town, there was only one school and likewise, there was only one bus to ride. Now he was all alone. But was he? Somehow he felt that Captain Dojure and Turlow were mounting the bus with him, and he took much comfort in this thought. If he could face pirates on the high seas and warrior jungle men by moonlight, surely each day he could face a bus ride without his siblings. And with that assurance, Jim stepped up on the bus to face his brave new future as a fifth grader.

Jim survived his first week at his new school. In fact, he even made a new friend, a boy his age who lived in the same neighborhood as he did. His friend's name was Charles Watson, but everyone called him Chuck for short. Chuck and Jim hit it off well, and in the ensuing months and years became quite attached. Regular peas of the same pod and all that. But Jim wondered if he could ever tell his friend about his "experiences," and if he did would his friend even believe him. Only time would tell.

Anel thoroughly enjoyed being a wife again, and she adored being home every day for the children. They were the light of her life. And soon a little more light would be added to her life. She just did not know it yet.

Although neither Brent nor Anel were expecting it, just before Halloween they found out that Anel was pregnant. However, they waited until Christmas Day to make the joyous announcement, because there were enough surprises this year already, with their marriage and having the kids move away from family and friends to Illinois. They felt this would be wise. Actually, they had no clue how the children would react, so it was a long month and a half trying to keep this huge announcement a secret. Anel's morning sickness was no help either.

Christmas finally arrived, and during the time that Brent was reading the Christmas story, sharing about the birth of baby Jesus, Anel decided to share about *another* baby that was coming. Except this one would not be born of a virgin in a manger, and he (or she) certainly would not be the Savior of the world. Nonetheless, this baby was still very important and special. Just as any being that possesses the human genome is acutely special.

It took the kids a few moments before they were able to connect the dots. Theresa was the first, and she was elated.

She threw her arms in the air, and exclaimed, "We're gonna have a baby!"

At this, Brent and Anel turned towards one another and exploded with laughter shaking their heads in approval. That is when it was completely obvious for John and Jim; there was no mistaking Anel's encrypted message now. Jim and John were sort of stunned. They were not upset or angry or anything of the sort. They were mainly shocked and were without words.

At this point, Jim thought to himself, "Wait, I am gonna have a baby brother or sister?" The thought seemed more like he was navigating a foreign language, rather than pondering some idea from his own reality. Either way, this *was* reality. Jim was no longer going to be the "baby" of the family, and he was not quite sure how he felt about that yet.

Anel and Brent tried to read the faces of John and Jim to see how they were going to react, because they had not said anything yet. At least they had not spoken anything out loud, because there was plenty being said within their own minds.

That is when Anel spoke up to the boys, and said, "Boys, are you okay?"

John spoke up first and said, "Of course, Mom. I'm just shocked. I'm excited for sure. Just shocked."

With that he got up and gave Anel and Brent a hug. Jim followed suit with the hugs, but still could not find any words to express his current state of emotions. That was alright. Brent and Anel took a hug as a good sign, compared to how Jim reacted to the news of their impending marriage.

That night, as Jim lay in his bed, pondering the news they received that morning, oddly enough the thought of a little baby coming into the family brought a smile to his face. In fact, the more he mused upon the thought the more he smiled. At last, he determined that he *was* excited about this news. He realized that, although he would no longer be the "baby" of the family, something even better was about to take place; he was going to be a "big brother." This was something that Jim never even imagined would take place in his life. Somehow this thought made him feel older and more responsible, and a sense of honor rested upon him. "I will have a baby brother or sister to take care of," Jim said to himself. And with this thought, Jim peacefully dozed off to sleep.

The next morning, at the breakfast table, Jim made it very clear to Brent and Anel, to the whole family really, that he was jubilant about this new baby, this new life, coming into the family and he expressed how he could not wait to find out if they were having a boy or a girl. Up until this point it was still a mystery. That mystery would still loom for some weeks.

Jim was excited for school to start, because they were in the middle of a study on World War II in his history class. The subject completely enthralled him. With his vivid imagination he could envision the battles, whether on sea, land or in the air. The idea of the *entire world* at war mesmerized him because being someone who did not live through that era; it was hard to wrap his mind around it.

Christmas passed and the new year began. School started back up in January, and the kids were back to school. Anel normally loved having the kids home on break but this time, with the pregnancy, she found it hard to muster the normal energy she so naturally exuded each day.

John and Theresa could not wait to get one step closer to graduation. Jim just enjoyed going to school and learning new things. He was in no hurry for it to end. He and Chuck had the same homeroom class and ate lunch together as well. So, for Jim, going to school meant he would be spending all day long with his new best friend. That suited him just fine.

One day as Chuck and Jim were playing after school at Jim's house, Jim tried to broach the subject of internal worlds with Chuck. "Hey Chuck, have you ever thought of travelling to a different world?" Jim asked.

"What do you mean? Like on a spaceship?" Chuck replied.

Jim clarified, "No, I mean like another *dimension*."

"Ohhhh, that would be so cool!," Chuck exclaimed. "But I don't know if I've ever thought about that. Not even sure where I would want to go to tell you the truth. Why, what about you?"

"Yeah, I think it would be pretty cool. I think about going to other worlds often. I even day-dream about it at school," Jim replied.

That was it. No more and no less. Jim had at least planted a seed in Chuck's mind. This was the first time he had any conversation about his unique adventures with another human being, since speaking with

Theresa and John at the genesis of these internal travels. Being able to at least bring the subject up with someone else brought some measure of comfort and relief. He was not quite sure why, but nonetheless it did.

Sometime in March, Jim came home from school one day, and Brent was home early from work. This was strange, because Brent was very punctual. He left for work at the same time each day and returned home like clockwork. On top of this, his mom seemed to be unusually gleeful. "Mom are you okay?" Jim asked.

"Oh, yes, dear. Just fine," Anel replied.

Jim did not believe her. He pressed further, "Well you seem *very* happy today is all."

"Well it is a *very* beautiful day. Why wouldn't I be happy?"

Jim knew that his mom was up to no good. He knew something was off kilter. He just shrugged his shoulders, and said, "Ooooookay."

He finished his after school snack and headed to his room to work on his homework. The sooner he could finish it the sooner he and Chuck could play basketball in the driveway. Chuck's family life was not too pleasant. His parents fought. A lot. So, they would play over at Jim's house most of the time. A few times they played at Chuck's, but when Chuck's parents began fighting it made it real awkward for them. Even though having a new step-dad was awkward for Jim, he knew it was not nearly as awkward as Chuck's situation. He felt bad for him, so he certainly did not mind having Chuck over to play as often as he like.

Today, playing would have to be delayed though. Because, when John and Theresa got home from school, Brent and Anel gathered the family in the living room. They were doing their best not to seem overly giddy, but the radiance from Anel's face betrayed their attempt to conceal their happiness.

As they sat in the living room, Anel spoke up and said, "Well, we have some news. We are having a boy!!"

The whole family was over-elated, and cheered and hugged all around. Theresa stopped everyone, and asked her mother, "Wait, what is his name?"

Anel, with much happiness, turned towards Brent and then back to everyone, and said, "Michael Brent." That night they all went out to eat to celebrate. They even brought Chuck along.

That was certainly a day that Jim would remember forever, because it was the day he found out that he was having a little brother. John and Theresa had always been very good with Jim. They occasionally teased him, like any older sibling would (or should) do, but there was nothing overly mean. They set a very good precedent for Jim to look up to and he was determined to be the best big brother he possibly could.

They visited a local Italian restaurant that night and everyone delighted in freshly made spaghetti with meatballs. It was a jubilant occasion for sure. Full of merry spirits and love all around. Even Chuck seemed excited about the news. More than likely, though, he was just glad to be around a family that was not fighting. It was a breath of fresh air for him.

The festivity was over and they all headed back home. They dropped Chuck off back at his house and said goodnight. Finally they reached their own home. It was already evening, and it was already past bedtime for Jim. Tomorrow was a school day, but thankfully it was a Friday. Jim lay in his bed reminiscing about the day's events. He thought of all that happened to his family that past year; from his mother's and Brent's marriage, to the move to Illinois, to the announcement of a baby, and now the news there would be another boy. It seemed like a lot to take in.

At some point during his mental musings, the thought of the other worlds and Fobos and all that comes with them pierced his mind. He wondered when, if ever, he would return to that other dimension. It was still very adventurous to Jim but after the last excursion, it was also much more evident that *real* dangers exist on the other side. Dangers that very well could spell certain doom for him the next time. And with this last thought, he drifted off to sleep.

School came to an end for the year, and the kids were very excited. The excitement did not solely stem from the reality of summer break but also came from the expectation of the incoming sibling. In just a few weeks they would all get to meet little Michael Brent. It was an interesting paradox because with all of the new changes and upheaval over the past months for the kids, the birth of this baby seemed to eclipse all of those uncomfortable things. Brent and Anel, despite their newfound love for and life with each other, in their own ways, still hurt from the loss of their spouses. This turned out to be a blessing in disguise for both of them because the baby seemed to be the needed salve for their wounded hearts. Summer was here. For Jim, that meant lots of swimming (and chores), and playing with friends (and more chores). For John and Theresa, who were now 16 and 15 years old respectively, that meant getting part-time jobs and hanging out with their friends when not working. John and a friend of his from school mowed grass together and Theresa got a job at a local theater. She worked the concession stand selling popcorn, candy, soda, and everything else that cavities so desperately love.

John wanted to buy a car that summer, so he worked very hard. Theresa just wanted extra money to spend with her friends when they went to the mall or shopping. Next year she would save up for a car herself. Jim was content being at home most of the time with his mom, because every day she would bake something absolutely scrumptious. And every day Chuck would come over and help Jim devour the delectable treats. Sometimes they were cookies. Sometimes they were muffins. Sometimes it was a pie. No matter what it was, it was sure to be eaten within minutes.

Anel thoroughly enjoyed and relished the fact that she was able to be home with her kiddos now that they moved to Illinois. She loved watching them grow each day, like a gardener carefully eyeing her tender plants each new sunrise. She counted it an enormous blessing in her life because for a number of years when she had to get a job outside the home after her husband's death, she absolutely missed being home with them. She was now thankful for the opportunity that God gave her and thankful as well for Brent providing the life they now had. Providence surely rested favorably upon her that past year.

July came and so did D-Day (Delivery Day)! That Monday morning started out like any other day. Brent left for work at eight. The kids came down for breakfast around nine. By ten, John and Theresa left for their prospective jobs. Jim did his chores around the house. He was tasked with cleaning the bathrooms and vacuuming the house each day. As well, he had to take the trash out. When his work was complete, he ran down the street to get Chuck, and they went back to his house to swim and play. Being near Chicago and Lake Michigan, Waukegan had a pretty moderate summer with temperatures in the eighties and lots of sunshine. It made for great times during summer breaks.

That day shifted quickly around one o'clock. Anel started having contractions, and she knew with past experience that those contractions *were not* Braxton-Hicks. These were the real deal.

"Jim, get in here!" Anel yelled out the window to the pool.

Jim jumped out of the pool and came quickly, because he recognized a good measure of anxiety in his mother's voice. He knew from what his mom told him that Baby Michael would be appearing any time now.

"Mom, are you okay?" Jim asked.

He had not bothered to dry off, so he stood in the kitchen dripping wet. Anel was sitting in a kitchen chair holding her stomach and working on her breathing.

"Get the phone and call Brent!" she gasped out.

Jim bolted towards the phone and dialed Brent's office.

The secretary picked up, "Borgins Law Firm, how can I help you?"

"Susan, this is Jim, is Brent there?" he asked in a very panicked tone.

"No, Jim. He's in court right now. Is everything alright?" Susan asked.

"No! Mom's having the baby. We need Brent to come home!"

Anel, realizing from Jim's conversation that Brent was *not* at the office, directed Jim to tell Susan to get in touch with Brent and tell him to just meet her at the hospital.

Jim relayed the information to Susan and hung up. "Now what do we do, Mom?" Jim asked frantically.

"Get Chuck. We need to have his mother take me," Anel said as calmly as she could. She did not want to give young Jim a heart attack. She had been through this three other times, so she knew she had *some* time. How much, though, she did not know, because with each subsequent birth it seemed that the labor portion of childbirth lessoned in length.

Jim grabbed Chuck out of the pool and had him call his mom. Within ten minutes, Carol pulled into the Borgins' driveway with her Oldsmobile station wagon. Carol helped Anel into the front passenger seat, and helped her get her seatbelt buckled, while the two boys, who still looked like drowned rats with towels wrapped around them, jumped into the backseat. Anel's labor intensified and Carol drove rather erratically. Anel tried to calm Carol down while Carol tried to do the same for her.

The boys, in the meantime, sat in the back seat, and were completely stunned at the scene unfolding before their very eyes. Neither boy ever saw anything like this in their lives, and from all appearances it seemed as if Anel was about to *die*, not give birth. They just sat in tense silence, hoping and praying for dear life. If Anel did not die, *they* would all surely do so, if Carol could not get her driving under control.

Thankfully, the hospital was not too far from their house, and thankfully Susan was able to get in touch with Brent. Brent was granted a recess by the judge to go attend to his wife and incoming son. He sped as fast as he could to the hospital, hoping he would not get pulled over. Although, he was an attorney, so he was not too worried if he received a speeding ticket.

Carol pulled up to the emergency entrance and quickly helped Anel vacate the car. You would think the two were comrades in the midst of a raging battle the way that Carol was so caringly helping Anel along the way. I guess two women sharing the communion of labor pains *does* make them comrades, minus the raging battle. At any rate, they made it to the hospital safe and sound. That was the most important thing.

The nurses immediately checked Anel in and Carol ran back to attend to the car. Oh, and the boys! The boys sat stunned in the back seat not exactly sure what they were supposed to do. They figured their best bet was simply to sit still and wait. Sure enough, their bet paid off, because Carol was relieved to see them still in the car. She pulled the car around to the parking lot and found a spot with relative ease. Waukegan was not exactly a metropolis.

Carol rushed back into the hospital with the boys in tow and the nurse at the front desk directed them to the labor and delivery department. As they made their way to the assigned area, Brent showed up. He rushed in like a sprinter finishing the final lap at the Olympics. He was out of breath and by all appearances seemed as if he would pass out. He simply bent over, took a few deep breaths, and then took the plunge into the labor and delivery department.

As he entered, he was not sure if he entered a labor and delivery department or a torture chamber, because of all the screaming and yelling. Although this unnerved him greatly, it certainly did not deter him.

"Borgins," he said to the nurse at the desk. She promptly gave him a face mask and cap to don and ushered him into Anel's room. Brent was a sight for sore eyes for her.

"Brent, you're here!" she exclaimed with such relief.

Meanwhile, back in the waiting room, Carol impatiently sat with Jim and Chuck. The boys still had wet swimsuits and were still wrapped up with their towels. Jim could not imagine what his mother was going through at that very moment. He was excited for this moment. He wanted to be a big brother. Now that the time arrived he was not sure how to feel. Their whole family environment was about to shift, and Jim was no longer going to be the baby. He thought he was alright with this, but was he truly? Time would tell.

He tried to envision what his mom was going through, and he hoped she was doing okay. He cared deeply for his mother and felt sad that he could not be there for her at that time. Even so, he knew that Brent was taking very good care of her because he loved her very much too. All Jim could do now was pray and ask God to help his mother. So that's what he did. Jim looked up to the heavens and like an archer with bow and arrow in hand, shot a short yet sharp prayer up, "God, please help my mother!"

After what seemed like an eternity, John and Theresa finally arrived. They found the note on the kitchen table, and made it to the hospital as fast as they could. Jim jumped to his feet and hugged them both, very tightly. Carol decided to take her leave with Chuck, since the rest of Jim's family arrived, and she knew he would be well taken care of.

"Jim, would you like me to grab you some dry clothes, and bring them back to you?" Carol inquired.

With a shiver and a nod, Jim replied, "Yes, please."

With that she rushed over to his house, and had Chuck run into their house to get some clothes from Jim's room. They dropped the clothes off at the hospital and returned to their home. Anel still had not given birth, but surely it would not be much longer. The screams were getting louder and louder.

Shortly after Carol departed, the head nurse popped in the waiting room to give the kids an update. "Your mother is doing just fine. She is dilated to seven centimeters. Won't be too much longer now," the nurse said in a reassuring manner. She had been through thousands of births. Most, simply (and most affectionately) refer to her as the *Grand Puba* of the birthing department. Rightly so!

John made a run to the hospital cafeteria to grab everyone some food to eat while they eagerly awaited the arrival of the extremely cute human creature. Truly children are a gift from God.

Jim was doing much better now that he was fully garbed. The food John bought for everyone helped as well. By now, the pastor and his wife from their church arrived to help support the family during this exciting time. Jim was very fond of the pastor because he was an elderly gentleman who happened to also be a World War II veteran. He shared many stories with Jim about his time in the war. He was a bomber pilot stationed in England during the war, and carried out many missions over Germany. He was one of the very fortunate to never get shot down, let alone survive the entire war!

The nurse informed the family that Anel was now dilated to nine centimeters and the birth would not be much longer. Everything seemed to be going along just fine. Soon they would embrace the newest member of their family. It was all so unnerving yet very exciting.

A short time later the atmosphere quickly shifted, and *not* for the good. From the waiting room, the family could hear nurses scurrying about. Then Jim heard the clear declaration over the intercom, "Code Blue." The nurses believed the umbilical cord was wrapped around the baby's throat, because the baby's heartbeat was dropping and fast. Anel was whisked away to the operating room like a soldier on a stretcher being evacuated from a battlefield. Brent would not be allowed into the surgery room, and had to wait with the rest of the family. He came in and explained everything to the family. Jim had never seen Brent look so terrified. And just like that this exciting moment turned into one great big nightmare, conjured up from the darkest mind possible.

Brent had been through one wife passing away, and he heard too many stories of women passing away from childbirth. He was a complete wreck, especially because he was not allowed to be with Anel. He was fine as long as he was allowed to be with her. The separation killed him.

Jim's mind was swirling and swirling like an airplane in a black spin. "What just happened? Everything was going so well. The nurse said that it wouldn't be much longer. How could this be happening?" were the thoughts bombarding Jim's mind. Then Jim overheard Brent telling the pastor and his wife that the baby's heartbeat was rapidly dropping along with Anel's blood pressure. Brent was trying to convey this to the pastor and his wife in a way as not to alarm the children, but children *do* know how to put two and two together. They are much wiser than most believe.

This news seemed to go off in Jim's mind like one of the atomic bombs dropped over Japan. His eyes froze straight ahead, and he fell back into his seat. "Does this mean the baby could die? Does this mean my mom could die? What does this mean?" were the thoughts with a death grip on his brain.

Jim was absolutely numb at that moment in time, and the prayer he shot up to God earlier seemed to return and pierce his own soul. As Jim sat corpse-like in his seat, a substance that seemed to be like fog began to envelope the entire waiting room. At first, Jim thought there was a fire, and they would have to evacuate. He wanted to panic, but no one else seemed to even notice the mysterious substance. The more Jim noticed it, though, the more it filled the entire room.

The foggy presence seemed to slowly, yet methodically, cover everyone and everything. First, the candy machine in the corner, then his brother and sister, then the chairs, then Brent and finally the pastor and his wife. The fog now enveloped the entire room. So much so that Jim could not even see his own hand just six inches from his face.

At that moment, terror seized Jim's very soul, and the only thing he could think to do in response was to yell. With his eyes closed and his white knuckles gripping the arms of his chair, Jim yelled at the top of his lungs, "aaaaaagggghhhhhhhhhhhhh!!!!" He thought that maybe this would grab the attention of those around him to signal his panicked state.

His yell lasted a good twenty seconds or so and in the duration he noticed something changing. Whether it was himself or his surroundings he was not sure, but he knew something was changing while he wailed. Although he did not want to open his eyes to discern the change, he would not have the luxury of such a decision.

"Lieutenant, quit your yelling. We've got to abandon the aircraft!" said Colonel Jones.

Jim looked out in front of him and all he could see in front of him were clouds and more clouds. He looked out the window to his right and he noticed two engines were on fire. "I'm on an airplane," Jim thought to himself. But before he could reckon any longer about his current state of affairs, Colonel Jones quickly reappeared in the cockpit, but this time he was not so cordial with Jim.

The aircraft was all shot up. All four engines were lost and they were losing altitude fast. They needed to don parachutes as quickly as possible, and jump while they could still make use of their current elevation. If they waited any longer, the parachutes would be nothing more than fellow meteorites along with every person on that aircraft. Jim did not know this was his current plight but thankfully the Colonel did.

Colonel Jones helped Jim out of his seat and back towards the fuselage. Jim noticed that Colonel Jones was already suited up with his parachute and there were four other men who did the same. Jim was the last one and they helped him into it lickity split. As soon as they were ready, each man took a rifle and one by one jumped out the side door of the aircraft.

Jim was lined up in front of the Colonel but before he jumped the Colonel said to Jim, "Don't forget to count to ten and then pull your cord!"

It was a good thing Colonel Jones said that because, in fact, Jim had no idea he should do that. He had never even stepped foot in an aircraft before, let alone jump out of one into the dark night sky with only some small pack strapped to his back.

Right before Jim jumped, though, he noticed that there were other men in the aircraft who were not as fortunate as he. They had already been killed by enemy fire. He also noticed the full extent of the damage to the wing and engines, at least on right side of the aircraft. They had already descended below the cloud line so right as Jim jumped he realized that not only were they jumping out of a burning aircraft with nothing but backpacks for reassurance, they were doing so at night.

Jim jumped out the door, and for whatever reason yelled, "Moooooommmmmyyyyy!" "One, two, three, four, five, six, seven, eight....oh forget it," Jim said in his head. Then he reached for his cord and pulled it as hard as he could with his right hand as he clung as tightly as he humanly could to the rifle with his left. When he did so, he could hear some type of material unfurling behind him, and then all of a sudden there was a hard jerk followed by an instant slowing of his descent.

Floating downwards, Jim noticed cannon fire piercing through the night sky all around him, and he saw other aircraft that were hit falling in the distance. Jim watched as their own aircraft plummeted into the earth. The smell of smoke filled the air. Within seconds Jim would be reaching the earth, but he did not even know what part of the earth he was on. To be honest, he was just guessing that he was on earth. For all he knew he could be on another planet!

As he descended farther and farther away from the clouds, Jim could make out there was a forest below him and that he was dropping straight for it. There was no way of avoiding this confrontation so he tried to brace for impact, pulling his knees up close to his chest. He just did not want to go slamming into the earth, since he did not know the slightest thing about parachuting, especially about landing.

As Jim's feet entered the top of the forest he could discern that these trees were very large pine trees and that their branches were very close to one another. When his parachute reached the trees, he lost what little lift it provided and his speed increased for a split second before it ceased all at once. The sudden jolt of his stop loosened his grip from his rifle and it fell from his hand. He watched it fall and land in some of the lower branches. Like a marionette in a puppet show, Jim found himself dangling in the tree line, unable to quite reach his final destination.

"Now what?" Jim thought. That's when he looked up and noticed Colonel Jones happened to be coming down right on top of him. All he could do was cover his head and hope and pray that the Colonel would slow down as he did so he would not come crashing into him. "Awwwwwwww," was the only thing Jim could hear as the Colonel entered the treetops. Jim heard branches snapping and popping with every inch of Colonel Jones' descent until finally there was nothing. At this, he looked up and the Colonel's feet were only six inches away from his head!

"That was a close call," Jim said to himself. He looked up at Colonel Jones, and even though he did not know his name yet, asked, "Are you alright?"

"Yeah. My plane's crashed, half my crew is dead, and we are now stranded in the tree tops of some God-forsaken forest in Nazi Germany!" the Colonel lamented. "Other than that, yeah, I'm fine."

Both men squirmed and writhed about, trying to loosen themselves from their parachute pack, but trying to do so in a manner that kept them from falling twenty feet farther which would more than likely injure them, if not worse. Jim discovered he had a pocket knife tucked in one of his pockets and began to slowly cut the straps. Apparently, Colonel Jones had had the same idea and was carefully cutting his own straps as well.

Before they finished, though, they heard voices below them. They saw flashlights and in the distance, heard dogs barking and growling as well. They saw two German soldiers pass below their tree and heard them talking as well. This was *way* too close for comfort. Jim and Colonel Jones instantly froze and could not even utter a breath. They knew these men were after them and if they were discovered, they knew that more than likely they would either be instantly shot or taken captive only to be tortured. The Nazis were barbaric in their treatment of enemy combatants, let alone civilians. This was a widely known fact amongst the allied forces during World War II.

After about five or ten minutes of hanging in complete silence, Colonel Jones whispered to Jim, "Let's try and get down now."

Within just a few moments, both men were free of their packs and stealthily climbed down the trees branch to branch. Thankfully these were very large coniferous trees so their branches easily supported their body weight. They made it down safely, but they were nonetheless covered in sap. At least they would taste extra delicious to the dogs if they were caught.

On their way down, they were able to retrieve both their rifles, which fell amongst the branches in their tussle to free themselves. Luckily, their rifles did not fall to ground, or else they would have surely been found out.

"Okay, Jim, is your mom having surgery really more frightful than being pursued by blood-thirsty Nazis?" Jim lectured himself.

Within a few seconds of Jim making it out of the trees, Colonel Jones was able to make it down as well.

The Colonel reached into one of his belt pouches and immediately loaded his rifle, so Jim thought it wise to follow suit. He watched exactly the steps the Colonel took, and he did likewise. Jim learned enough from the other times he "went within" to catch on quickly to those around him, as to ensure his chances of survival increased exponentially. So far, so good.

He and Colonel Jones were locked and loaded, and in whispered tones began to formulate a plan. They knew the other men were in the area, but where and how far spread out they did not know. This was mainly wishful thinking, because the truth was the chances of them a) surviving the jump and b) not getting caught by the Nazis who were crawling everywhere, were slim to none. But they had to remain positive about it. They had to at least hope *in* hope.

Since the Colonel was the last one to jump, he at least vaguely saw with what little moonlight was protruding through the clouds, the direction the other four men landed. It seemed, to the best of the Colonel's knowledge, based off the direction they were flying and the place where they landed, that he and Jim landed about a kilometer east of the other men.

The Colonel worked out a strategy for him and Jim to stay in the covered forest area as long as possible, as they worked their way west in search of their comrades. The two remained spread about ten meters apart. This way each had a different vantage point, helped cover each other better, and if the enemy caught one, it made it much easier for the other to escape, if he could escape at all. Jim knew he was pretty quick, but up against a German Shepherd? Well, let's just say he was not so convinced of this in his mind.

As they crept through the wooded area, they were doing their best not to step (or breathe) too loudly. They realized that the bombing raid was still in full effect, and the loud concussions of the bombs being dropped by their fellow pilots could still be heard from where they were. This was a tremendous help because it provided some needed sound cover for their search and rescue mission.

Every once in a while, the Colonel, knowing the risk of his actions, shined his flashlight up into the trees to see if any of their buddies were still caught up in the trees. Fifteen minutes into their search, they came across some parachute packs on the forest floor. This was the first sign they came across of their fellow crew members.

However, as they searched the pack, they realized this was not an American pack; it was a British pack, so they figured that it belonged to some other chap who abandoned his aircraft on an earlier run as well. The odd thing, though, was that the pack had all its contents in it: food, water, and even a pistol. Then, as they searched the pack, they discovered it had a map. This was a total God-send for sure, because they knew they were in northern Germany. However, when they parachuted out of the aircraft they did not know their exact location. For some reason, jumping out of an aircraft at 15,000 feet in the fog (at night to boot) seemed to have that kind of effect on their geographical bearings, even for highly seasoned pilots such as Colonel Jones.

Their end target was the town of Stuttgart. That is where their entire squadron of bombers was tasked with bombing on that run. They knew the time it would take for them to get there based on airspeed calculations, the elevation they would be flying, and the aircraft's total weight with crew and payload. As the Colonel perused the map, he knew they only had another ten minutes of flight time to reach Stuttgart, so that gave him a general idea of where they were. By his estimation, they parachuted into the northern end of the Black Forest. This newfound knowledge was both comforting and terrifying at the same time.

It was comforting, because they at least had some notion of their general whereabouts. On the other hand, it was terrifying, because they realized they were *trapped behind enemy territory*. Despite all the advancement the allied forces made by this time in war, Germany still had a very tight grasp of its own country's borders, and right now they acted like a ferocious sow, who was backed into a corner defending her cubs.

They gathered the supplies from the British pack, put the map away, and continued on their search mission. They had four other crew members to still find, and it was very cold out. Germany was no fun place to be outside in the winter of 1944. They continued their silent trek through the woods with all their wits about them. They were very nervous because they were seriously outmanned and outgunned in the enemy's very own backyard. Not a good position to be in to say the least.

As they crept along, they heard a twig snap above them. They instantly froze and knelt down, and the Colonel shined his light up into the trees. It was one of their crew, but sadly he did not make it down alive. More than likely the impact in the trees broke his neck, and he was hanging completely limp in the large tree branches.

Colonel Jones had Jim climb the tree to retrieve the airmen's supplies and weapon, as well as retrieve his dog tag. They would not cut him down, because they did not want to give any evidence that they were there if the enemy happened to stumble upon his body lying in the forest, which was very possible with all the dogs they heard earlier. When Jim got to their crew member, he could definitely tell he was dead, and he realized that his supplies (and weapon) had already been stripped from him. As quickly as he ascended the tree, he descended, because he wanted to alert the Colonel.

As he landed, someone stepped out of the dark with a rifle pointing right at them, and all they could hear was, "Don't move or you're dead!"

The Colonel instantly recognized the voice, and knew it was one of his crew.

"Lowe, is that you?" the Colonel quickly questioned.

"Yeah...is that you Colonel?" the figure in the dark shot back.

"Yeah, put your rifle down," Colonel Jones shot back.

They all huddled together in the dark forest to review their situation. The Colonel went first, "The Lieutenant and I were the last to jump, and we landed right on top of each other in the trees about a kilometer east of here. From what I could see, the rest of you landed around this area, and we have already seen German soldiers and dogs searching the area. As we were hanging in the trees, trying to get out of our packs, two German soldiers walked right beneath our trees, and thankfully they never heard or saw us!"

They explained to Lowe how they came across the British pack with supplies, and how they retrieved a map of the area. They also explained that they believed they were in the northern end of the Black Forest, about ten minutes' flight time northwest of Stuttgart. At this point, Lowe shared everything about his own landing.

He said that he and Johnson landed near one another, and Lowe was able to get down from the trees rather quickly. He heard Johnson land in the trees, and he heard him land with a pretty rough thud. When he went searching for him, he saw him hanging in the trees, so he decided to climb up to check on him. That is when he realized that Johnson broke his neck upon landing, so he decided to strip his supplies yet leave him hanging for the very same reason that the Colonel and Jim were going to leave him in the same state.

Lowe continued and shared that he started making his way west to search for any of the others, when German soldiers appeared in the forest. That is when he saw them capture Frankie and Irish (as they were affectionately known by their crew). Great! Their search mission just turned into a search *and* rescue mission, further complicating their entire dilemma, but they knew that anyone of them would at least attempt to rescue the others, if they found themselves in the same plight.

The Colonel ascertained from Lowe that the soldiers took Frankie and Irish towards the south. They figured there was some outpost nearby, and surely there would be a road as well. Even though the Germans were, as a whole, fiercely defending their own borders, the Colonel knew that *morale* as a whole was very low amongst the German ranks as well. They hoped this would play to their advantage with their new mission.

They needed to move quickly, because the sun would be rising soon. This would dispense with *most* of their cover, even though the forest still provided for a good amount of that, even in the daytime. They were bitterly cold but they could not build a fire (no matter how much they longed to warm themselves) for obvious reasons. Staying on the move helped keep them warm for now until the sun rose in the morning. Hopefully the fog would dissipate enough to allow the glorious sun rays to burst through, provided the immensely dense forest mercifully allowed some of those same rays to penetrate to these pitiful, chilled soldiers.

The Colonel reasoned in his mind that they were no longer a flight crew. They were now an infantry crew, whether they liked it or not, and they needed to conduct themselves as such if they had any chance or hope of survival as well as rescuing their comrades. This reality caused them to fall back on their skills they were taught in basic training, because, when you take a pilot's wings away, he (or she) instantly becomes what everyone else in this bloody war was...a soldier! And so their new mission commenced.

Chapter 5 - Operation Unplanned Rescue

Colonel Jones knew that this mission posed great risk to himself and the remainder of his crew. He also knew that any of his crew would undergo the same mission. War has a way of doing that to comrades, so that each one is willing to die for the other. In his mind, the Colonel knew their mission was two-fold: somehow rescue Frankie and Irish and somehow make it across the Rhine River into France. The allies advanced far enough into France that he knew it was their best bet. Really, it was their *only* bet.

The only thing they knew at this point was that the Nazis took Frankie and Irish and headed south. So that is the direction they headed. The woods were thick and dark, which made travelling during the day easier, because it provided some necessary cover for them. However, the snow was another story. It was now November and the snow did much more than blanket the countryside. It brought the entire bed with it. They had the cover but they did not have the speed, and this was certainly not ideal for a rescue.

As they anxiously traipsed along the forest floor, Jim's mind wandered back towards reality and the thought of his mom in surgery came to the forefront. Here he was facing life and death in Nazi

Germany while his mom faced possible death with a complicated birth. He could not help but take notice of their parallel situations. He also realized that in school they had been covering World War II in his history class, and for the first time he connected the dots between that which he was taking into his mind and that which he was currently experiencing. This fact opened his eyes to the connection that was there these past five years.

Jim was still trying to process the reality he just figured out between his internal world and his real world when Colonel Jones came alongside him.

"Lieutenant, how are you holding up?" he asked in a quiet tone.

Jim replied, "Better than can be expected, considering our present circumstances, Colonel. I'm just grateful to be alive. How about yourself, sir?"

"At first, I could not believe that I actually had to abandon my aircraft, and now I can't believe that I am *walking* through Nazi Germany, instead of flying," the Colonel humorously said. Then the Colonel asked Jim a very embarrassing question, "So, Lieutenant, when you jumped out of the aircraft, did I really hear you yell, "Moooommy?"

Jim's face was already red from the cold, but the red compounded at this question. To his chagrin, his head sunk as he nodded.

"Well, your secret is safe with me, Lieutenant. Just know that you owe me," the Colonel said in a reassuring tone as he patted him on the back.

Still unable to make eye contact with the Colonel, Jim replied with an awkward, "Thanks."

Sgt. Lowe was several meters in front of Jim and the Colonel. He was scouting out their route while Colonel Jones and Jim kept an eye out for any Nazi troops in the area. They were trying their best to stay in the woods as long as possible because it was their best chance of coverage while travelling during daylight. However, they knew this coverage would need to end soon, because they needed to utilize a road or a railroad track soon to try and track down Irish and Frankie as quickly as possible.

****

"Captain Fobosen," a young German sergeant said as he saluted the officer. "Our men have captured two American troops. We believe they were part of the air raid last night on Stuttgart and their aircraft was shot down."

The Captain was staring out of the window of his office smoking his pipe as the soldier relayed the news to him. After the soldier gave his report, there was an awkward pause of silence between the two men and the sergeant felt very uncomfortable. He was not sure if the Captain heard him, and he was not sure he wanted to interrupt him if he was thinking.

The Captain was notoriously ruthless to everyone, even to his own men, especially to those he deemed as disloyal. And his definition of loyalty shifted often, depending on the situation they were faced with at any given moment. With this type of reputation preceding him, it was no wonder the sergeant decided to quietly wait for his officer to reply rather than restate his report.

Finally, Captain Fobosen slowly turned around to face the young German soldier and as he did, a puff of smoke travelled with him. At first, the soldier could not even see Fobosen's face from the pipe-induced cloud, but as soon as the cloud lifted, the soldier finally caught a glimpse of those menacing eyes the Captain was equally infamous for. A pair of eyes so grimacing they seemed to pierce your very soul with every glance. However, Fobosen's eyes were all the young Sergeant could see, for he had some type of leather mask covering most of his face. The Sergeant wondered, "Why does he have a mask on? Is his face burned?" He deemed it wise not to verbalize his thoughts.

"Where are they?" Fobosen slowly questioned.

The sergeant replied, "We've taken them to the outpost at Ettlingen to be processed and questioned."

With this, Fobosen said one simple word, "Gut! That will be all sergeant. You are dismissed."

As soon as the sergeant left his office, he called for his assistant, "Corporal!"

At this, the corporal swiftly entered the room and with a salute said, "Yes, Captain."

Fobosen replied, "Get my vehicle ready. We are going to Ettlingen to pay a visit to the Americans being held there." The corporal replied with an affirmative and promptly left to do his captain's bidding.

Captain Fobosen was a part of the *Schutzstaffel* (or the SS as they were infamously known), and his unit was stationed at Karlsuhe, a small town in southwest Germany, which was right up against the Rhine River. They were tasked with a very specific mission: shoot any and all German people and/or soldiers attempting to flee to France to

85

surrender to the Allied forces. Oh, and while they were at it, torture and kill any captured Allied troops as well. A very ignoble and dastardly mission to say the least, but one in which Fobosen reveled.

The corporal quickly readied Fobosen's vehicle, and within minutes they were speeding towards the captured American troops. Only God knows what was going through the Captain's mind, what menacing thoughts he was entertaining for those poor, detained soldiers. Hopefully Colonel Jones, Jim and Sergeant Low would make it in time to not only save them, but make it across the Rhine into France as well. Forces were now set in motion that could not be avoided. They could only be faced.

For Jim and company, they first needed to find out where Irish and Frankie were taken, and then figure out a way to get to them. That meant they had to find some German soldiers near them, the one thing they were trying to avoid. Unbeknownst to them, they landed in the Black Forest near the town of Spielberg, which was just southeast of Ettlingen. From where Captain Fobosen was travelling and where Colonel Jones' crew was, Frankie and Irish were in the dead middle. The only good news in all this was at least Ettlingen was on the way towards the Rhine.

They were walking for some time now, and they decided to stop and get a bite to eat. Thankfully they were able to scavenge some of the supplies from their fallen comrades, because it provided some much needed sustenance. Their sacrifice would not be in vain. As they sat in the Black Forest, each man leaned up against a tree as they snacked.

Lowe looked at Jim and said, "How you holding up LT?"

Thankfully Jim deciphered that Lowe was speaking to him, because the Colonel called him Lieutenant earlier. "I'm doing alright. The jump from the airplane last night shook me up pretty good, but I figure it could have been much worse," Jim replied.

The Colonel chimed in, "You've got that right. Even in this hell hole, it is still a blessing to be alive."

Lowe asked the Colonel, "So, what's our next move, Colonel?"

Colonel Jones replied, "Well, I know this seems crazy, but we actually need to find the closest German soldiers. Somehow subdue them and ascertain the whereabouts of Irish and Frankie. Hopefully they are not too far away from us." With that, they finished eating their food and gathered their gear to keep trekking onward.

As they walked in a southeasterly direction, they finally came across a road. It was rudimentary at best, but nonetheless it was a road. Sgt. Lowe took the point, and Colonel and Jim spread out to keep their eyes open. They crept up to the edge of the road to have a look around. Jim and Jones covered him on each side. Lowe looked to the right and there was nothing but snow covered trees on each side of the road. As he turned to his left, there was something entirely different. There was a small guard outpost several hundred meters up the road. He could not make out exactly how many German soldiers were there, but from first look it did not appear to be a great number.

"What do you see?" Colonel Jones asked.

Sgt. Lowe stealthily crawled back down into the forest, and shared, "The bad news is there is a small outpost of German soldiers just a few hundred meters to the northwest. The good news is there is a small outpost of German soldiers at the same location."

Both Colonel Jones and Jim looked dumbfounded at Lowe before Colonel Jones said, "Okay. How many are there?"

Lowe replied, "I am not 100% sure. We'll need to move closer to know for certain."

"Okay, let's move out," the Colonel ordered. And off they went, tracing the route of the road while trying to still utilize the forest coverage.

They walked for about fifteen minutes before they decided to take another look at the outpost. Sgt. Lowe crept up to the edge of the road while the Colonel and Jim provided cover for him. This time Lowe took the binoculars with him, and they were close enough for him to obtain a much clearer situational report. As he peered through the binoculars, he saw two guard shacks, one on each side of the road with a lifting roadblock bar to stop any vehicular traffic for inspection.

Lowe slid back down the edge of the road towards Jim and Colonel Jones to divulge the newly acquired information, and he relayed the situational report to them. With that, Colonel Jones came up with the plan to create a diversion, so that they could take on the German soldiers. Since they were outnumbered, a diversion was definitely necessary, especially since the Germans were on each side of the road.

The plan was to sneak up as close as they could to the guard shack on their side of the road, use one of the grenades they acquired, and throw it deep into the forest on the other side of the road to draw all the guards' attention away from their side. At that moment, they would seize the guards on their side of the road, and take out the other two guards across from them. It was a good plan. Now it was time to implement it. Here went nothing.

Jim was slated to create the diversion, so while Sgt. Lowe and the Colonel crept up to the shack on the western side of the road, he prepared to throw the grenade at their signal. Once Lowe let loose two whistles Jim, from the cover of the woods, like an ancient catapult, leaned back and heaved the grenade as hard as he could across the snow-covered dirt road into the trees. Kaaaabooommm! The guards all dove for cover. Now there was no turning back.

Colonel Jones and Lowe immediately pounced on the guards near them, striking them with the butt-ends of their rifles, and telling them to freeze. Meanwhile, Jim was tasked with taking aim and taking out the far two soldiers.

"What am I doing?" Jim asked himself.

As his comrades wrestled their captives into the guard shack, the other two guards opened fire on them, exposing themselves to Jim. He knew that this was his moment and that if he did not seize it, his comrades would be in immediate peril. He took a deep breath, aimed his rifle, and *bang*! He hit the first soldier, wounding him yet not killing him, and he quickly took aim on the next one. He duplicated his last action with fierce precision, and the guards never knew what hit them.

By this time Lowe and the Colonel had their captives hog-tied with their own belts and boot laces. Jim ran to them to see if they were alright. Then Colonel Jones and Lowe went to check on the downed guards across the road while Jim kept a rifle on the tied-up captives. They knew their time was short, so they moved quickly.

One soldier was already dead while the other one was shortly approaching death's door. They dragged both of their bodies into the forest about thirty feet away from the guard shack to not leave any evidence near the road. They stripped off the guards' uniforms, and changed into them. Colonel Jones and Sgt. Lowe were going incognito.

There was a military truck at this checkpoint, and Colonel Jones came up with a great idea. They would hold the other two German soldiers hostage, and have them lead them to the base at Ettlingen, where Frankie and Irish were being held, and help them get into the base. They would pretend to hold Jim hostage, as if he were *their* American captive. The Colonel would ride in the front with one German, holding him at gunpoint as he drove them to the base, while Lowe and Jim rode in the back of the truck with the other German. The plan was sound, but would it hold up?

Jim and Lowe crawled into the back of the truck with their captive, and pulled the cover down. Jim had a pistol in his jacket in case either he or Lowe needed to quickly deal with their captive. Colonel Jones loaded up in the front with his captive, and pointed on the map where he wanted the soldier to drive to.

"Ettlingen," he said. He asked the soldier, "Gut?"

The soldier gave a short nod. And just in case he was to get any funny ideas, the Colonel made sure he knew he was pointing his rifle right at him.

The young, scared German soldier, who could not have been more than eighteen years old, started the engine and they were off. The trip would be bumpy, especially for those in the back, but it would not be very long. All their butts were very thankful for this. Little did they know, though, that as they drove along Captain Fobosen just arrived at the base in Ettlingen. Time was ticking.

******

As Captain Fobosen approached the gate, the soldiers saluted him and without hesitation, opened the gate for him. They all knew him (and his mask), or at least they knew *of* him, and his infamous reputation preceded him everywhere in the German army. They knew he was stationed there to deal harshly with friend or foe, any who opposed the Third Reich.

The gate opened and the Captain's driver speedily pulled the car through, and drove straight to the base headquarters. Upon entry, the base commander, Colonel Strauss met with Fobosen. He saluted the Colonel, "Heil Hitler!"

The Colonel returned the salute in kind, "Heil Hitler!"

"You are here for the Americans, no?" Colonel Strauss questioned the Captain.

"Yes, where are they being held?" he quickly responded.

"Well, we have much more pressing news to talk about beyond two piddly Americans," Colonel Strauss commandingly said. He continued, "The allied forces are right now mounting a force to traverse the Rhine. By this time tomorrow, they *will* cross the Rhine, and will swiftly make their way towards Karlsruhe on their way to Frankfurt. That, Captain, is the situation we face, and my advice to you is to forget about these two Americans."

"Thank you for your advice, Colonel. Respectfully, though, my orders are very clear, and I will not shirk from them in the face of the enemy" he decidedly said.

Even though the Colonel out-ranked Captain Fobosen, the Colonel was not a part of the SS. The SS trumped all other branches of the German military because they were akin to Washington's *Immortals* during the American Revolution: a group of soldiers devoutly, if not religiously, serving their leader, no matter the impending outcome of the war. Except the SS were ruthless, immoral, murdering dogs, trying to exterminate an entire race, and Washington's *Immortals* were trying to fight against political tyranny. In both cases, though, these groups were closely held in high honor by both leaders, which meant they also received special treatment within the military.

At this, the Captain stood up and said, "Please direct me to the American dogs." The Colonel hesitated, because he knew this was neither the way to conduct war nor treat captured enemy combatants. Although he was a highly decorated member of the German military, he had never joined the Nazi political party, because outside of the military he was a *Baron*. He was a wealthy landowner, who was patriotic, but not fanatical. There was a clear difference and the differences were presently personified by these two soldiers.

"I am sorry, Captain Fobosen, but these Americans are under *my* command. The Americans will be here by tomorrow, and I will turn them over to them. We will treat them in accordance with the Geneva Conventions, just as we would expect the Allied Forces to treat our captured soldiers. I am sorry to disappoint you after making the drive here. My decision is final," Colonel Strauss firmly said. He continued, "Now you and your driver may drive back to Karlsruhe at first light."

At this Captain Fobosen asked, "Are you German or American?" He then drew his pistol and shot the Colonel in the left leg.

"Aaaggghhhh," Colonel Strauss yelled in agony as he collapsed to the floor while he gripped his wound. "You mad man!" Strauss yelled at him as he writhed in pain on the floor. The office door flew open as Captain Fobosen's driver and another soldier bolted in to assess the situation.

"The Colonel is wounded. He is relieved of his duties. I am now in command of this outpost," Fobosen declared. Then he said, "Bandage his wound and help him to his quarters. Make sure you lock his door."

"Yes, Captain," the two soldiers quickly responded. They wrapped a bandage around his bloodied leg, helped him to his feet, and carried him to his room as he hopped on one leg.

After Captain Fobosen had Colonel Strauss locked away in his room, he posted a guard at his door and he directed the soldier who helped his driver to take him to the American captives. The soldier quickly answered, "Yes, sir!" And off they went.

*****

Meanwhile, Colonel Jones and his crew neared the outpost at Ettlingen.

"Schnell!" Jones shouted to the driver, because he wanted him to put the pedal to the metal. It was one of a few select German words that he knew, and he figured it was a great time to make use of it. At this, the soldier floored it as he plowed his way through the south-side of the town. The base was on the south-side of the Alb River as well, so it made it easier to get to.

Colonel Jones lifted the flap to the back and told the other two, "We are almost there. Get ready. Keep an eye on that guy. I don't want any funny business giving us away." At this, Sgt. Lowe put his hand to his mouth, and said, "Shhhhh." The soldier nodded in agreement.

It was dusk now, which they hoped would work in their favor, so that the guards at the entrance to the outpost would not be able to get a very clear view of them. Their hope was that their driver would quickly get them through the gate but once they got in, they had not the slightest idea what the next step was. They were flying by the seat of their pants right now and this was not such a bad thing, since the Colonel had much experience doing just that!

Just as Captain Fobosen was entering the building where Frankie and Irish were being held, Colonel Jones and his men were pulling up to the gate. The driver said some words in German, which the Colonel did not know, but one word he was able to decipher was "Amerikaner." Jones was watching the faces of the gate guards to see if they had any suspicions. One guard waited by the driver's door, while the other went around to the back to make sure. The soldier lifted the rear flap, and shined a flashlight at the men.

The German soldier pretended to hold Jim captive while Sgt. Lowe quietly held his rifle to the soldier's back, so he did not blow their cover. The gate guard asked the soldier a question, and he answered him back. Just like that, the soldier got down, went back to the other gate guard, and relayed a positive response, "Gut!" At this the third gate guard opened the post gate, allowing their truck to pass through and as they passed, one of the gate guards told the driver where to pull his truck. Surely fate was on their side.

As they parked the truck, the sun set and the cold German night grabbed hold. Although it was cold, the night sky was clear and bold. You could see many stars in the sky, and hopefully Orion and his bow would give aid to Colonel Jones, Jim and Lowe with their rescue operation. God knows they needed all the help they could get. Unbeknownst to them, however, they would get the needed help from much closer than distant galaxies.

*****

Captain Fobosen had the post soldier lead him to Frankie and Irish's cell, and, after looking at them in disgust, he ordered them to be brought to the "interrogation room." It was clear, though, that he had no intentions of interrogating them. This man was sadistic, and wanted these Americans to feel the full brunt of his evil pleasure.

Fobosen removed his hat, uniform coat and tie, and had his driver fetch some tools to assist them in their malicious endeavor. He was brought a knife, a hammer, and welding machine. Frankie and Irish were brought in by two other soldiers, and were immediately tied to chairs. They saw the torture tools laid out, and knew where this was going. They quickly ascertained that this was *not* going to end well. Colonel Jones and his crew had only minutes to save their comrades.

Outside the prison building, there were two soldiers standing guard, so this posed the first obstacle they needed to hurdle. Their hope was that their German captives would still play along, but it was a gamble at this point, since they were no longer in the Black Forest; they were now in the lion's den. Their mission stood on the edge of a knife at this point, and only time would tell which way it would turn.

As they disembarked from the truck, Captain Psycho (Fobosen) began his torture by slowly tracing the razor sharp knife up and down Irish and Frankie's arms, so they had blood flowing down each arm. In just a few minute's time, their arms looked like they had been turned inside out. It was a gruesome sight. Both men, although very strong and brave, reeled in agony at the pain.

Their hands had been tied to arms of the chairs as well, and Fobosen decided to have some fun with the hammer for a few minutes. He wanted them to feel pain equal to the evil he felt in his heart, and with that wish he broke both their hands. Irish and Frankie howled in misery at this point, and could hardly keep from passing out from the pain.

*****

Colonel Jones felt the urgency, but he could not let this betray them before they got into the building. They approached the building guards, and the driver spoke similarly as he had to the gate guards. Jones frightened him enough that he figured the young man did not want to lose his life for nothing. At this, the guards ushered them into the building and directed them where to take the prisoners.

As they walked down the dank, narrow hallway following one of the building guards, they heard the screams of their comrades. Their shrieks pierced their souls to the core. They knew they were close to them, and that their plan was working. But how to execute the rescue *and* make it out of the base alive was still as an enigma to them. This is where Colonel Jones finally decided to just make a move and hoped his men would follow him.

Before they reached the prison cell, Jones whacked the soldier in front of him in the back of the head and shot the building guard, who was leading them, in the back. As quick as lightning, Sgt. Lowe followed suit and knocked out the other soldier with his rifle as well. They dragged all three men into a prison cell, and used the keys off the building guard to lock the door.

They had to backtrack a little towards the hallway where they heard the screaming come from and as they did, they were not sure what resistance they would encounter. Captain Fobosen had his driver and the post soldier standing guard outside the interrogation room. When they heard the shot, the driver stayed while the other soldier went to investigate. The Captain was too engrossed with inflicting pain on Frankie and Irish to notice the gun shot a few moments ago. By now, he had broken both of their feet as well, and the blood streaming from their arms was painting a sad picture on the floor beneath their chairs.

Sgt. Lowe proved to be a great point man on the dirt road, so he again took the lead. They made it to the hallway where they heard the screams coming from, and headed down it. No guards so far. As they came upon another hallway to the left, Lowe cautiously peered around the corner and when he did, he saw the German guard coming their way. He immediately motioned for them to stop and take cover in the room adjacent to them. As the soldier rounded the corner, Lowe shot him, and they dragged him into the room and closed the door.

Captain Fobosen's driver heard the shot, and was now frightened enough to open the door to alert the Captain. "Captain, someone is here. They are shooting!" he said in a very alarmed tone.

The Captain, with pure evil burning in his eyes, stood there covered in blood from his devilish activities as he held the welder in his hand. He was entering phase three of his torture plan before his driver interrupted him. This very much aggravated him, and he responded by shouting at his driver, "Well, go and find out what it is!"

The driver turned to go and inspect, and just as he was shutting the door behind him, Sgt. Lowe shot him through the chest. He fell back into the interrogation room and now even Captain Fobosen was greatly alarmed. He dove behind the Americans to use them as a shield.

Right at that moment, Colonel Jones heard aircraft overhead and no sooner did they hear them than they heard the sounds and rumbles of bombs falling all around them. This was the bombing raid to soften the German defenses before the allies crossed the Rhine River the next day, although the Colonel did not know the latter part.

They all ducked down, because they did not know if their building would get hit. All of a sudden a bomb landed just outside the prison and ripped through its structure. The concussion rocked them all and much of the building simply crumpled. The blast knocked Frankie and Irish's chairs back on top of Captain Fobosen, knocking him unconscious and pinning him to the floor underneath a good deal of rubble.

Up until this point, Jim had not really thought of his mother in the hospital or his life back home, but as he lay underneath the rubble, his mind wandered back to his normal reality. He could see his mother in the hospital. He could see Brent and his brother and sister along with their pastor in the waiting room. They all looked so concerned and anxious. He could tell their hearts were very heavy. He keenly sensed this in the atmosphere. Then, as he saw all this in his mind, he then saw himself lying in a hospital bed, and this last picture startled him. "Why am I lying in a hospital bed?" he questioned. At the present moment, he did not know the answer to this question, but he did know that he needed to make it home *alive*.

Jim began stirring from the rubble. The sound of bombing could still be heard (and felt), but it seemed much more distant at this point. He began to call out to his comrades, "Colonel, Lowe, are you all okay?" As he called out, he pushed up through the rubble to get a view around him although the darkness, which now enveloped them, was no help at all.

A faint groaning could be heard, and Jim called out again, "Colonel is that you?"

"Lieutenant, give me a hand." The Colonel could barely get the words out of his mouth. The concussion from the blast slammed him very violently against the wall in the hallway. It was amazing that he was alive. Jim moved towards the voice, and eventually was able to feel a hand sticking out of the rubble. At once he began clearing the rubble to get to Colonel Jones.

Within a just a few minutes, he was able to free the Colonel from his entrapment, and they were now in search of Sgt. Lowe. Thankfully, Colonel Jones had a flashlight in his pack, and was able to bring some light to aid their search. The blast had been powerful but since they were all pretty close to one another before the blast, there was only so far away that Lowe could have been thrown.

They located him near where the doorway to the interrogation room had previously been located. Sadly, there was no response. After vigorously prodding and calling to him, they could not get any reaction from him, and when the Colonel felt for a pulse, there was none to be found. He was a brave soldier, and it is very likely that Jim would not still be alive without the efforts of Sgt. Lowe. Jim could feel the sadness welling up in his heart, and a couple of tears streamed down his cheeks. He was very grateful for Lowe's sacrifice.

As he knelt beside the now departed Sgt. Lowe, he and the Colonel could hear the cries for help from Frankie and Irish. Panic struck them both because like a boomerang returning to the very hand that flung it, the reality of their rescue operation came back to the forefront of their minds.

Immediately, the Colonel shined his light towards the sound of the cries, and he and Jim rushed towards them. They set up the flashlight so that it provided the necessary light for their work, and they began clearing rubble as fast as they could.

The Colonel said out loud, "We didn't make it all the way here for these guys to die! Clear faster!"

Within a few minutes, they saw both comrades, and they perceived the dismal state they were in. Even though the Colonel and Jim's hands were cut and bleeding from clearing the rubble with no gloves, their wounds at the present moment were nothing compared to that of their comrades' injuries.

They cleared all the rubble away, and gingerly cut them both free from the chairs that Fobosen bound them to. They could see that they were in horrible shape, and they did not want to injure them any further while trying to free them. Then, as they helped them up from the chairs, Jim saw someone under some of the rubble, behind where they cleared Irish and Frankie. So, he carefully set Irish down and while the Colonel looked them both over, he went to investigate.

He cleared some of the rubble away from where he saw the person, and he assumed that this was the maniac who inflicted such pain and torment on his comrades. Curiosity gripped Jim and as he was clearing more of the rubble away, he saw where the guy's head was. For some reason, Jim just *had* to see his face but when he cleared the rubble from his face, Fobosen's mask frightened him. So much so, that he let out a yell, "Aaagghhhh, the mask!" as he fell back on his butt.

"What is it?" the Colonel asked.

"A man with a mask on," Jim exclaimed. He thought to himself, "Isn't this the same guy who has tried to kill me every other time now?"

Colonel Jones asked Frankie and Irish, "Is this the guy who did this to you?"

They both simply nodded, because they were still too overwhelmed to speak.

"Is he alive?" the Colonel asked Jim.

"I don't think so. There's no movement at all, and I don't hear any breathing," he responded.

"Alright, leave him there, and let's get our guys out of here. We still have to figure out how to get out of here without being shot," the Colonel said in a worried tone.

Jim and the Colonel were able to provide some minimal bandaging for their comrades, and help them to their feet.

"Guys, I know this is going to hurt like nothing else, but just lean on us. We're gonna help you get to the truck," the Colonel reassured his men. He was helping Frankie and Jim had Irish.

They made it back to what used to be the hallway, and the Colonel lead them back through where they first came. The rest of the building seemed to be in better shape from where they just came. Once they made it to the main hallway, where they initially came in, it was a straight shot to the truck. Frankie and Irish were in really bad shape, though, so it was definitely slow going.

As they approached the door, the Colonel had to set Frankie down for a moment, so he could look outside to see what their situation was. As he looked outside, it did not look good. Their truck was turned on its side and was burning. It was completely demolished by the bombing raid, and the sounds of the same raid were still heard all around them. This was unnerving, because there was no certainty they would not be hit by another such bomb. It would be a sad affair to go through all of this work and danger, only to succumb to fratricide.

The Colonel went back inside, and said, "Well, the good news is I don't see any German soldiers around. The bad news is that our truck is blown up. Either way, we are going to have to get out of this building and commandeer a new vehicle. Let's move." With that, they made their way out of the crumbling and now half-blown up prison building, stepping into the dark, cold German night. Even with all the fires from the bombing, the darkness was difficult to penetrate.

The Colonel remembered there was a vehicle at one of the main buildings as they came through the gate. So he decided to lead his men towards it in hopes that it would be there, and that they would not be shot along the way. It was about a 300 meter trek to the building, and, with the shape their comrades were in, it would not be a quick one.

After ten grueling minutes, they made it to the building (or what was left of it) undetected, and the Colonel set Frankie down again to go see if the vehicle was still there. It was! Now they hoped they could load up quickly enough to get away. There was no top on the vehicle, and it only had two doors. Jim and Irish got in the back, and Colonel Jones helped Frankie into the front passenger seat. Then he bolted to the driver's door and got in, only to find out there were no keys.

"Dang it, no keys!" the Colonel yelled. "Well, I guess it's time to revert to my youth when I used to steal cars," he said.

Jim was in the back trying to keep an eye out for any trouble. Although he was not sure what he could do, since they lost their rifles in the rubble. Maybe he could shout them away?

As the Colonel was doing his best to jumpstart the vehicle, they heard a German accented voice yell, "Halt!" They all froze because they knew they were all exposed. Jim was keeping an eye on their rear, but the voice came from behind him, from the building they were parked in front of. He instinctively put his hands in the air, and was too frozen to even turn around.

The Colonel slowly sat up and raised his hands in the air as he looked in the direction from which the voice came. As he did, he could see the silhouette of a man leaning on some type of stick coming out of the front door of the building. The man approached the vehicle, and, as he did, it was apparent the man was seriously injured since he was limping on his left leg.

The man slowly and cautiously approached the vehicle. As he did, after he saw it was the Americans, he exclaimed, "You are the Americans!" I thought you were Captain Fobosen. He is the one who shot me. That mad masked-man. He is not even a man. He's an animal."

It was Colonel Strauss. When the bombing raid hit his building, it blew his door open, freeing him from being locked in his own room. Once he regained consciousness, he made his way out of the building, and that is when he ran into Colonel Jones and his men.

"Do you know where you are going?" Colonel Strauss asked them.

Colonel Jones answered, "Not exactly. And we lost our weapons too."

At that, Colonel Strauss replied, "Have your man run inside and there are several rifles in the main foyer. They will serve you well." Jim jumped out of the vehicle, ran into the building, and grabbed the rifles. Just as he was exiting the building, he heard the engine of the vehicle start up, and knew it was time for them to go.

He jumped in the back again, and Colonel Strauss finished giving them directions. "I am so sorry for what happened to your men. I tried to stop Captain Fobosen, but as you can see he would not be stopped."

Colonel Jones said, "Thank you, sir, for helping us," and with that he put the vehicle in reverse. As they backed away from the building to turn around, a gun shot rang out, and Colonel Strauss dropped to the ground. Panic struck Jim's heart, as Captain Fobosen and four other soldiers raced around the corner of what remained of the headquarters building.

Colonel Jones wasted no time putting the vehicle in drive and flooring it. Shots rang out towards them, and Jim returned some shots in kind. They continued to fire at them as they rushed toward the gate, as Jim laid down cover fire. There was no way they were stopping to open the gate. They were going straight through it.

"Duck!" Colonel Jones shouted.

Jim did just that just as they plowed through the front gate. The gate guards responded too late to stop them, but Jim fired a couple shots to keep them inside their shacks just in case.

Even though they sacrificed a man in the process, Jim and Colonel Jones made it out of the German base alive, somewhat beat up, but nonetheless alive. Frankie and Irish were in very bad shape, but they were thankful to be alive as well. A few more minutes alone with Captain Fobosen and that would not have been the case. Now they needed to make it across the Rhine River without being shot by their own men.

Colonel Strauss gave Colonel Jones general directions to get to the Rhine, but when they got to the river he was still not sure what their plan should be. He was still flying by the seat of his pants. So far, it was working well for them.

As the Colonel flew along the road, headlights appeared in their rear, and Jim knew it had to be Captain Fobosen and the soldiers from Ettlingen.

"Colonel, we've got company!" Jim yelled at the top of his lungs so the Captain could hear him over the roar of the engine.

"What?" Colonel Jones responded.

Jim turned around, sat up near the Colonel, and said, "That masked-maniac is on our tail. We're running out of time."

Colonel Jones was going as fast as he could considering a lot of the roads and the town were just bombed out during the last air raid. There was considerable dodging and weaving going into his driving right now. This did not help Frankie and Irish at all, but hopefully, at the end of this ride, they would be back in the hands of the Allied Forces.

The headlights were gaining on them, and with the light of the fires along the road, Jim saw that they were being chased by two side-car motorcycles. When they got close enough to their car, the shots started ringing out.

"Keep your head down, Colonel," Jim yelled. Jim saw Fobosen driving the front motorcycle, and he was brandishing a pistol, which he certainly made use of when he could. Their journey to the Rhine just got even more dangerous with the *SS* trying to take them out.

Unbelievably, even amongst all the chaos, Colonel Jones spotted a road sign for the Rhine, and abruptly turned towards it, almost flipping their vehicle in the process. Jim, in the meantime, returned fire at the soldiers chasing them.

"How you hanging in there, Jim?" the Colonel asked.

"Doing good. Still trying to pick one of their guys off," he replied.

"Great. Just don't be calling for your mommy," Colonel Jones exclaimed in a joking manner.

Jim laughed, "Yes, sir," and continued to fire.

They were running low on ammo. He had already switched to the second rifle, and was not sure how many more bullets that one had. Finally, he was able to pick off one of the motorcycles, as he shot the other driver. Captain Fobosen, however, like a vampire after fresh blood at night, was still in pursuit.

Another sign for the Rhine appeared and this time it said they only had two kilometers to go. This was good news, but Fobosen was closing in on them. He had already shot out their tail lights and shattered the windshield. At that moment, he shot out their rear left tire, and, as the rim hit the road, Jim flew up and out of the vehicle. He hung on the driver's side, on the outside of the vehicle, as the Colonel sped along. He knew they lost a tire but he was not aware that Jim was hanging on for dear life.

He happened to glance in his side mirror, and when he did, he saw Jim hanging on for dear life. Irish was in no shape to help Jim, but nevertheless he was over there helping pull Jim back into the vehicle. All the while Fobosen and his goon were still letting bullets loose at them. Despite the immense pain in his broken hands and cut up arms, Irish was finally able to pull Jim back into the vehicle, just as they approached the river.

Colonel Jones saw the bridge in sight and without hesitation gunned the vehicle straight for it.

"I'm out of bullets," Jim yelled, and it was likely that Fobosen and his man were out too, since the bullets stopped whizzing by at this point. Fobosen realized they were all out of ammo, and proceeded to get his motorcycle right up to the bumper of their car. Colonel Jones was zigging and zagging around large holes in the bridge from where artillery blew huge chunks away.

Fobosen's goon jumped on the rear of the car, and he and Jim were now in hand to hand combat as they wrestled furiously. The German soldier had his hands around Jim's neck as he tried to strangle him on the trunk. In their tussle, both of them slid into the backseat, with the German soldier still on top of Jim. At that moment, Colonel Jones ran over a very large bump, and as the car popped back up, Jim used his legs to push the soldier off him. As he did, the soldier went flying out of the vehicle and over the side of the bridge.

"Auf Wiedersehen!" Jim yelled.

Just as he got rid of the German goon, Captain Fobosen rammed his motorcycle into the rear of the vehicle, jolting everyone inside. This threw Colonel Jones for a loop and the vehicle spun out of control, and they slammed into the sidewall of the bridge, leaving half of it on it, with the other half dangling over the Rhine. At the same time, Fobosen's motorcycle flipped over as well. He did not care if he lived or died as long as the Americans died.

Colonel Jones banged his head on the steering wheel and was unconscious. Jim was completely spooked, but he was awake. He saw the predicament they were in, and wondered why Fobosen had not got to them yet. The vehicle sat on the side edge of the bridge like a children's teeter-totter. Except this teeter-totter provided zero amusement for all involved.

Jim knew he had to help his comrades get onto the bridge quickly before the car dropped into the river, but he knew he also needed to do so in the most careful manner as not to imperil them. He figured they needed to offload the front passengers first, while he and Irish kept enough weight in the back to keep the car from tipping over the side.

With as little movement as possible, Jim reached for Colonel Jones and shook him while shouting, "Colonel Jones, are you okay? Colonel Jones, wake up, wake up! We've got to get out of the vehicle before it drops into the river," he continued. "Frankie, are you okay?" Jim asked.

Frankie stirred somewhat and said in a very low and painful tone, "Yeah, I'm okay." This was certainly a positive development.

Just then Colonel Jones began to rouse a little as well. "Ohhhhh, my head hurts," he said. He examined his head, and after touching his forehead, realized his hand was covered in blood. The headlights of the vehicle were still beaming out in front of the vehicle, but it was too dark to make out anything.

"Where are we? Did we make it?" the Colonel asked.

"No, Colonel, we are hanging off the bridge, and if we don't get out of this car, we are going to drop into the Rhine."

To this, the Colonel responded, "What's your plan?"

"I need you and Frankie to come our way and get out first. This way our body weight will help keep the vehicle from tipping over the edge. Once you guys are out, then you'll help us get out," Jim said.

"Frankie, are you ready?" Colonel Jones asked.

Frankie nodded that he was, and with that Colonel Jones got on his knees and turned towards him. He carefully helped him into the back seat. Once he was there, the Colonel crawled back there himself, and then he and Frankie crawled over the backseat and onto the bridge. The Colonel helped Frankie sit down against the sidewall of the bridge, and then quickly helped Irish out. Just then, the vehicle started to teeter and tip over the edge. Colonel Jones dragged Irish out, and like a cat jumping out of a bathtub, Jim lunged from the backseat onto the bridge pavement. It was not a graceful jump, but it was one that kept him alive.

They all took a moment to take a breather, and gather their wits about them. They saw that Fobosen's motorcycle was flipped on its side about fifty feet back, and they were not so inclined to go inspect it. "Alright y'all, let's get a move on. Hopefully, we won't get shot by our own guys as we get to the other side," Colonel Jones said.

Jim helped Irish to his feet, while the Colonel helped Frankie up, and they started on their way to the other side of the Rhine by foot, all the while shouting, "Don't shoot, we're Americans! Don't shoot, we're Americans!"

They hoped that soldiers on the other side would hear them and not mistake them for German soldiers.

As they yelled for their lives, they were unable to hear anything behind them, and unbeknownst to them Captain Fobosen survived his crash. He crept up behind them with a knife. Through his coat, Jim felt a slash across his back, and cried out, "Ahhhh!" He dropped Irish and fell to the ground. Colonel Jones quickly dropped Frankie and rushed Fobosen as hard as a former line-backer could. He drove the Captain back to the edge of the bridge, and in their tussle both men went over the side wall.

Jim was mortified. "Colonel!" Jim yelled. He hopped to his feet and ran towards the edge as fast as he could. "Colonel, Colonel!" Jim continued yelling, hoping upon hope that he was still alive. No answer came, and Jim knew he needed to get Frankie and Irish to the other side.

As he turned to start helping them, several vehicles approached at a very rapid pace with headlights shining in their faces. Jim raised his hands in the air, even though the pain in his back was excruciating, and he yelled, "Don't shoot, we're Americans!" As the vehicles drew near, he kept yelling this, but he felt himself about to pass out from his wound. Just as the vehicles reached their spot, Jim collapsed onto the pavement.

The next thing he heard were muffled voices saying, "I think he's waking up. He's moving around."

Then he heard someone yell, "Nurse, nurse, help! He's bleeding!" At that, Jim blacked out again.

Chapter 6 - Time Marches On

O kay. You need to forgive me, for I must be honest with you. This chapter will be quite drab. There is no way around it. Despite its lack of excitement, it is still crucial to the success of our story. I *must* fill you in on some information, so that you are not lost. Just think of this chapter as an intermission, or a half-time show, minus the show. But you prefer to be thrilled, right? Well, I understand, but you cannot have your cake and eat it too. You will not get your "golden-goose" now. Sorry. Oh, I know you will forgive me.

So, where are we now and where are we heading? Good question. Well, Anel survived her emergency caesarean section, but since she lost a lot of blood during the whole episode, she remained in the hospital for almost two weeks after the surgery. She gave birth to a strapping young lad, little Michael Brent.

Jim, on the other hand, perplexed *everyone*. From what his family knew, he passed out in the waiting room from the stress and fear of his mother's situation, but when he did not respond to anyone after quite some time, he was admitted to the hospital since they thought he went into some type of seizure-induced coma. For over two days he lay in this state and just as they thought he was coming around, the knife cut from Captain Fobosen caused his back to bleed into the sheets of his hospital bed sending everyone into a panic, since no one could explain where the cut came from. Thankfully, Theresa noticed it quickly enough to call for help, and the hospital ably treated his injury.

Anel was torn, because she could not really get up. On one hand, she had a newborn to nurse, and she needed to rest her body. But on the other hand, her little boy was lying unconscious with a cut on his back in a bed in the very same hospital. She longed to be with him and comfort him.

Once Jim passed out on the Rhine River bridge, though, he came back to consciousness in his reality. The next morning he woke up, and the first thing out of his mouth was, "Mommmm!"

Brent rushed to comfort him, and assure him his mother was fine. He also made sure Jim did not move too much, as to not split his stitches open.

The nurses and doctor came in to examine him, and he seemed to be very healthy and doing well.

"Can I have some breakfast, please? I am very hungry," Jim stated.

"You sure can, partner," the doctor said. "Nurse Williams, could you please see that this fine young man gets some food?"

Within fifteen minutes, Jim had a scrumptious morning meal brought to him, and he devoured all of it, leaving not one crumb behind.

Brent just stared at Jim in amazement, because he was still flabbergasted at his whole ordeal. Thoughts raced through his mind, "Why did he pass out? Where did the cut on his back come from? What if this happens again?" He thought it best to keep these questions to himself for the time being until he and Anel had time to speak to him together. There had been enough drama for one week. He was just thankful that Anel, Michael and Jim were all alive *and* well.

After another day, Jim was released from the hospital and he immediately went to visit his mother and see his baby brother for the first time. Anel hugged him tightly, though not too tightly due to his back injury, and she just cried. Finally, Jim was able to see Michael, and when his eyes first lit upon him, he could not believe such a small creature could possess such magical powers, for, to him, the baby cast a spell on him, not allowing him to take his eyes off him. In other words, he could not believe how unbelievably cute his little brother was.

Brent eventually took Jim home, so that he could begin recuperating. Chuck and his mother, Carol, came over that afternoon to bring him a plate of freshly baked chocolate chip cookies and to check on him. Finally, John and Theresa came home from work and were very excited to see their little brother out of the hospital. Although both of them were very suspicious of the mysterious way in which Jim was injured.

When Brent was out of living room, Theresa spoke up first, "Jim, what in the world happened to you? Does this have anything to do with that sea-weed junk a few years ago?"

He did not know how to respond to her, because how does one begin to explain such a phenomenon, anyhow? He was in mid-chew at the moment, enjoying one of the delicious cookies from Chuck's mom, when Theresa posed her question. Before the words finished leaving her mouth, he about choked on his cookie. It did not help at all that John, who was sitting right next to him, tried to help him by patting his back, forgetting that that is exactly where Jim's stitches were located. Still trying to fully clear the cookie crumbs from his throat, he now wrenched upward in pain from the rough pat on the back.

All of the commotion caught Brent's attention from the kitchen, where he was trying to prepare dinner for everyone, so he shot back into the living room. "Is everything alright?" he asked with great concern.

John and Theresa's faces went pale, because neither of them knew how to answer. Now they were in *Jim's* shoes. Jim survived the cookie and the pat on the back, and thankfully, the whole incident drew his brother's and sister's attention away from their original question. Afterwards, he went to his room and fell right to sleep. The next week Anel and little Mikey came home from the hospital, and the family was reunited. The storm subsided. The waves calmed. Time marched on.

Weeks turned into months and months merged into years. Eventually, John and Theresa graduated from high school. John joined the U.S. Army as an infantryman right after graduation, and shipped off to Fort Bragg for basic and advanced individual training. The following year Theresa graduated, and earned a scholarship to the University of Chicago, where Jim would eventually follow in her footsteps.

Finally, around the time Mikey was heading into second grade, Jim finished high school. Then, he too, won a full scholarship to the University of Chicago, where he planned to pursue a degree in Political Science. Through the years there were other trips inward and other battles against Fobos, and each time Jim managed to escape and evade the foul clutch of his mortal enemy. However, these perpetual battles wore him down and drove a wedge between him and those around him.

That leads us up to the present time for Jim. You see, we have arrived back where we started. He was just hit by the city bus in Chicago as he and Lauren walked to dinner. Now, as the curtain is drawn back, we shall witness the final act of Jim's fateful story.

Chapter 7 - The Castle in the Mountain

Jim sat still for what seemed to him like hours, because he was mortified to stand up to see where he actually was. Everything seemed to be a blur at the moment. "Am I dead? Or did I travel within again?" he wondered. On top of this, his whole body tremendously ached, as if he had been hit by a bus. Well, truth be told, he had been, but not in this world. Despite the overwhelming pain, his curiosity got the better of him, so he slowly sat up. This proved to be difficult, though, because he realized that he was no longer wearing his jeans and t-shirt, he was clothed in armor.

"Your Majesty, are you alright?" one man asked him with a concerned look on his face.

He kept trying to get Jim to look him in the eyes, but all Jim could do was look at the men and the scenery about him. They were in a valley, full of luscious green grass which butted up against a grand forest with trees as tall as the buildings in downtown Chicago. This forest surrounded and blanketed the foot of a truly magnificent set of mountains. The entire view was more than one mind could process at the moment. It was truly a heavenly vista.

At last, Jim looked this man in the eyes, and replied, "I am alright. Thank you. Please help me up," Jim asked.

With that, the entire group of men, all at once, lifted him to his feet with great care and respect.

"What happened?" Jim asked them.

"Your Majesty, we were returning from our scouting run, riding along the valley back to the castle, when your horse was startled by a badger, sending you crashing to the earth. We feared the worst, but thank the Giver you are well. Despite what we discovered today, we will have much to celebrate tonight." The man said, "Let's ride."

With that, the entire troupe mounted their steeds, and finished their trek back to the castle.

As they approached the castle, Jim beheld its glory and splendor. It was no mere castle with a moat and an alligator with a rickety drawbridge as most would envision. Like Michelangelo's *David*, this castle was hewn right from the very sentry mountains which stood watch over it. The outer wall was a half-moon shape with each end subsumed into the bookended mountains. From above, the kingdom and the mountains formed a most amazing eye. There were eight towers along the outer wall, each resplendent in its own right, but behind this glorious wall, lay the main castle which was birthed over a thousand years ago from the very rear and most powerful mountain, *Delores*, named for the people's proto king. And now this entire kingdom bore the same name.

Rising from the middle of this castle, like a magnificent and stalwart giraffe overlooking the African savannah, stood the *King's Tower*. From there, the king overlooked the people and kingdom he was tasked with protecting and providing for. Unbeknownst to Jim, at this moment, was the fact that *he* was this people's king, and as providence had it, this was his dominion.

A roaring, crystal clear river named Lunaba lay before the splendid kingdom of Delores. Its sound was that of a thousand horses encircling the mountains and the city itself. The beauty of this river was almost beyond description, and it was as if the mountains filled this river each moment of every day from their very own cups, supplying its life from somewhere beyond the heavens. Not only was Lunaba breathtaking in scope and breadth, she also provided the outer defense for Delores. A grand meadow was spread out between Delores and Lunaba. Here the kingdom grew their fruits and vegetables, and each year the harvest was very bountiful. This year, however, there would be no harvest. The sounds of mirth and dancing would be fleeting.

As impressive and spectacular as the kingdom of Delores was, the impending war against the Caldans and their King, *Fobe*, took the very breath out of the city, for all knew this would be a devastating battle for all involved. The kingdom of Delores, in its vast and proud history, had never been breached, but the collective foe soon coming against it may well undermine that fact. Even so, the entire kingdom was preparing for this fight.

All the times Jim entered his internal reality, he always had someone there to guide him, to watch over and protect him, but not this time. This time he must guide and protect those entrusted to his care, all the while staying alive himself. This would be a turning point in his life more than he could imagine.

The horsemen swiftly approached Lunaba and crossed over the beautifully arched bridge, which seemed to be crafted by the very hand of God. It was as if the bridge and the ground were one, a sublime blend of stone, dirt, trees and grass. Because of this, the horses never truly knew they were crossing over the river. To them, it seemed as if they were merely leaving the valley and entering the meadow before approaching the Great Gate.

Ah, the Great Gate. How does one put into human terms the breadth, height and depth of such an imposing and marvelous edifice? The Great Gate was the sole entryway in and out of Delores. There was no moat before this grand entry for there was no need of one. Who needs a moat when you have Lunaba before your front door?

Two of the eight towers of the outer wall were on either side of the Great Gate. Each stood watch over the land, like uncompromising sentinels keeping guard over that which is most precious, every life within its walls. Each tower rose 100 feet in the air, which to any of us is an exceptional height, and yet their height paled in comparison to the towering mountains that overlooked the city.

At any rate, anyone entering the Great Gate would certainly be impressed, and every first time visitor to the city-kingdom was completely astonished. The size and scope of the gate was so hard to comprehend. Most people paused in bewilderment before actually trying to enter through it. As the horsemen approached the city, Jim did just that. His horse went from a gallop to a slow walk and finally it just stopped in its tracks as he beheld the city's glory. Most of the other riders around him did not notice at first, but the ones that did stopped with him as well.

"Your Majesty, is everything okay?" they inquired.

Jim sat there on his horse as he tried to grasp the enormity of this gate and everything that lay beyond it. Never, in all his trips around Chicago, had he encountered such grand architectural feats.

"Yes, I am fine. I am just admiring the beauty of this gate and the people and this great city," he somberly replied.

The men looked at him in wonder, because he spoke as if he never saw any of this before. They did not know that he had not.

Jim thought to himself, "This is the second time I've heard them refer to me as 'Your Majesty.' Why do they keep doing that? Am I their king?" The question pierced his mind like an arrow shot through an apple on a stump. "If so, does this mean that this is my kingdom?" he further mused. This last question almost sent him into cardiac arrest, but it was a good thing he did not keel over right there and then, since there were certainly no paramedics around!

Then, all of the sudden, he went from astonishment to curiosity. "Well, if this is my kingdom, then I ought to go in and see it," he said to himself, trying to muster the courage to keep riding forward. With that, he gave his horse a gentle kick on the side with his heel, as he said, "Yah." The horse galloped forward toward the gate, and the rest of horsemen followed suit.

He was not sure where to go once inside the gate, so this would be interesting. Thankfully, two of the riders took the point, and began declaring in loud voices, "Make way for the king! Make way for the king!" At those pronouncements, as they rode by, people began to clear the streets and kneel before Jim. This was a strange concept for Jim because in real life he lived in a democratic republic, where no one bowed before the other. Rather they all honored and respected time-honored text enshrined in a constitution. This would take him some getting used to, but he needed to do it quickly. Time was of the essence. In a very short period of time, he needed to acquaint himself with his new-found position, take in the full scope of his kingdom, and prepare to battle a foe beyond count or measure. A rather tall order.

The two front riders led the rest of the group to the horse stables, where they all promptly dismounted, and the stable workers put the horses away and provided food for them as well. Jim was careful getting off his steed because his body ached and throbbed. With that pain, the memory of what just took place, while walking with Lauren to dinner, with the purse robbery and the collision with the bus all flooded his mind. "Oh my God, did I really get hit by that bus?" Jim thought to himself as he lifted his leg over the horse. Then his thoughts turned toward Lauren and he wondered if she was okay. "She is there with me, if I am still alive, and I am here without her. I'm not sure which is worse."

His men could see that he still grimaced from the pain of falling off his horse, so they helped him out of his armor right there in the stable. The main soldier who helped Jim off the ground earlier returned to the stables, and Jim heard the men speaking with him.

"Sir Traegan, King Jimban is still in a great deal of pain from his fall."

Well, now Jim knew the name of at least two persons in this world: his own and this helpful soldier. Now he just needed to fit the rest of the pieces of the puzzle together. At least the fall gave him an excuse for seeming somewhat absentminded for the time being, and he planned to take full advantage of that until he could fully understand the world in which he presently found himself. As always, the primary goal for Jim with any of these travels was to survive.

Meanwhile, in the land of the Caldans, King Fobe just finished making a pact with the other two kingdoms of Eredia. There were four kingdoms in total. The Caldans, the Deloresans, the Pampans and the Thuldans. A thousand years ago, before all of the lands of their world broke apart from one another, there was a great earthquake which rent the lands away from each other and with each passing year they moved further and further away. When this happened, nobody knew how many separate lands were created by this great catastrophe.

At that time, the land of Eredia was inhabited by four main families, and at that time the families made an agreement with one another to divide the land equally amongst them. The Caldan family took the south, the Delores family opted to stay in the north, the Pampa family went east and, finally, Thulda and his family travelled west. And that is how it was for over a thousand years, and through those many centuries each family built their own kingdom.

There has been great peace between the kingdoms all this long while. That is, until King Fobe ascended the throne of the Caldans, because his heart was corrupted with greed. He was not content with only possessing one kingdom. He greatly desired to acquire *all* the kingdoms of Eredia, and eventually to go in search of the other lands to conquer them as well. First, though, his sights were set on the kingdom of Delores, for he envied them most for they were the only kingdom beset amongst such beauty and grandeur. In fact their kingdom was the only one on Eredia to possess mountains.

King Fobe's plan to deceive the Pampans and Thuldans into joining his plot was to conjure up a false report that the Deloresans were plotting to overthrow the others. In order to make this plan believable, though, the words needed to come from that of a *Deloresan*, not from his own lips, or else all would see through its thin veneer. If that happened, it posed grave consequences for his own head.

But, who would betray his own people and king? He heard whispers of a knight, Sir Laedo, amongst the court of King Jimban, who had some disagreements with the king. It was widely known, and this relationship was a source of consternation for the king and his court. It did not take much convincing by King Fobe to lure Laedo into his plot. He promised Laedo a spot at his side, great wealth, and a chance to usurp the very king he so disliked.

Fobe coaxed Laedo to tell the emissaries from the Kingdoms of Thuldan and Pampan that he had personally heard and seen a plan conceived of by King Jimban to conquer the other kingdoms by turning them against one another, and at which time, his army would swoop in to overpower them. King Fobe sent word to the Pampans and Thuldans, and requested an urgent council be convened for a most pressing matter. Nothing seemed unusual about that request, so each kingdom acquiesced and sent high ranking members of their court to the council. As they met, Sir Laedo presented the supposed evidence and false report to all the representatives and since it was coming from a member of the court of Delores, it was much more believable. Once Laedo finished speaking, King Fobe, building on the fear created by this news, roused a desire to exact vengeance on King Jimban from the other members of the council.

The men from Thulda and Pampa looked to Fobe and asked, "What are we to do? Since it is you who have brought this troubling news to our attention, what is your counsel?"

With this question, King Fobe had the other kingdoms precisely where he desired them to be: in the very palm of his hand. He then proceeded to lay out what he thought was their best recourse, given such terrible news. His plan called for the other three kingdoms to unite under one banner, with him at the lead, of course, and that they would march upon Delores to overthrow King Jimban. "Once we unite and subdue this treacherous king, we will divide up his land amongst our kingdoms, so that his treachery will never rise again in our peaceful land," Fobe slyly said to the council.

His real plan was to use this war as an impetus to turn the other armies against their own kingdoms as well. Once they all conquered Delores, he would already have the other armies under his command, which would make it much easier to follow through with his malicious intentions. And it seemed that the other members of the council were gullible enough to unwittingly follow him. With this one council, a thousand years of peace was sacrificed on the altar of concealed greed.

"Then it is settled. Within one month's time, at the time of the next full moon, we shall march upon Delores, and put to sword all those who would oppose peace in Eredia," Fobe declared. At that, the whole council rose with jubilant cheers and exuberance. That night they all feasted together, celebrating an unknown deceit. The only ones with true cause for celebration, however, were Fobe and Laedo, for their plan succeeded beyond all hope. Now they hoped their vile plan would come to fruition. A lot could happen in a month's time.

Back in Delores, Jim, or King Jimban as he was known by his subjects, was de-armored, and was led into his palace. Everywhere Jim looked his breath was taken away by the amazing designs of the buildings, the windows, the extravagant water fountains and especially how the city's architecture was so intertwined with land of Eredia. The grassy soil seemed to blanket every edifice, as if it were a blanket bringing comfort to a child. It was as if the land itself fashioned this city-kingdom and invited the people to live in it.

It was dinner time, so Jim was lead into the great hall in the palace. Over fifty people joined him at the table, and there was such a splendid array of food and drinks at the table that Jim found it almost impossible to eat. Everyone stood by their chair, waiting for Jim to reach his, and nobody sat down until he did. Just the sight of all this scrumptious food seemed to satiate his appetite. His stomach begged to differ that the sight of food was not sufficient, causing his mouth to salivate, which prompted his hands to bring the food to his mouth for consumption, which his stomach believed was a very wise decision. Jim agreed.

As they ate, Sir Traegan, who was seated to Jim's right, stood and proposed a toast, "To King Jimban. We are glad you were not hurt worse today."

With this, the rest of those at the table all stood, and in unison said, "Here, here!"

To which Jim raised his glass as well, and they all drank together. The musicians were seated along the wall opposite the enormous fireplace, and they began to lightly play while the king's court dined together.

Traegan sat back down, and, turning towards Jim, asked, "How are you feeling Your Majesty?"

"Sir Traegan, I am feeling well. Your concern for my wellbeing is most comforting," Jim said in almost unbelief at the austere words coming from his own mouth. He thought to himself, "I sound like an old man."

That evening he would soon find out just *how* old. Jim knew that each time he entered his inner world he was a number of years older than he was in real life, but this time, the disparity between his real age and his inner world age was at its greatest.

Jim leaned towards Traegan to speak privately, "You will forgive me, Sir Traegan, but I do believe that my fall today has muddled my memory a bit. I do not recognize these people right now."

To this Traegan replied, "I understand, Sire. You had a very hard fall today, so hopefully tomorrow you will begin to remember. In the meantime, I will help you remember those around you."

At this he winked at the king, and he and Jim laughed. They resumed their eating. After some time, despite the merry gathering, Jim with a full stomach and still aching was ready for sleep. He stood up and announced, "I shall retire for the evening. Thank you." At this, the entire room stood up, and Sir Traegan led Jim to his room.

When they entered his room, he and Jim sat in chairs in front of his fireplace, and Jim asked him to clarify who he was and where they were. Traegan was very gracious towards the king, and kindly and patiently explained to Jim that he was the king of Delores, in the northern lands of Eredia. He explained to him that he used to be married to a beautiful woman, named Juliosa, many years ago, and that she was unable to bear children. He further explained that after only ten years of marriage, she contracted a deathly sickness, and passed away. Traegan shared how he was heartbroken by her passing and that he decided to never marry again, thus leaving himself no heir to inherit his throne.

Traegan then went on to explain to Jim the dire situation that currently befell the kingdom, and how Sir Laedo betrayed their kingdom, treacherously co-hatching the plot with King Fobe to overthrow their people. "So, you see, your Majesty, within a few weeks' time, an army of immeasurable strength and number will fall upon our city, and we must make haste and prepare for this impending war."

These last words out of Traegan's mouth, "impending war," landed heavily upon Jim's ears and mind. He thought to himself, "Not again. These battles are relentless, and this masked maniac unceasing!"

As they sat in the chairs before the warm fire, Jim realized that he was smoking a pipe. He did not know how it got it in his hand or even how it was lit, but he figured it was probably out of rote memory from his present life. Jim stared at the inviting fire while he puffed on his pipe as he pondered the information Traegan presented to him.

In wonder, Jim asked Traegan, "Is there no one that we can call upon for aid?"

"In Eredia, no. But beyond the shores of our land, possibly. The problem is that no one from Eredia has ever made any contact with the people of the other lands since the great earthquake tore our world apart. We do not even know where the other lands are located or if there were any other survivors from such a disastrous event. For all we know, the peoples and kingdoms of Eredia are all that is left in our world."

Traegan did a superb job explaining the kingdom's detrimental position, but the thought of other lands with other peoples who could possibly help their people certainly piqued Jim's interest. "You said 'We do not know where the other lands are located or *if* there were any other survivors,' but we don't know the opposite either, correct?"

Traegan paused before answering, "That is true, your Majesty. What do you suggest we do?"

Jim responded, "We must send out our best sailors with our swiftest boats. Finding the other lands with the hope of finding any other survivors to come to our aid is our only hope. It would be foolhardy for us to *not* try."

The next morning Sir Traegan, along with Jim, gathered the war council together for a kingdom deliberation. "Fellow Deloresans and honorable knights of King Jimban's court, we know that Sir Laedo has betrayed our king and our people. He and King Fobe of Caldan have devised this wicked scheme to unite the Pampans and Thuldans with the Caldans to make war against our great people. Yesterday we returned from our trip. We met secretly with emissaries from both the kingdoms of Thulda and Pampa to try and persuade them to turn aside from this madness. Our meeting was to no avail."

He continued, "The plans and schemes of King Fobe had already tightly wound its tentacles around their hearts and minds. Even when our great King Jimban pleaded with them, explaining that we held no malcontent towards their kingdoms, they still would not relent. War is now upon us, whether we would have it or not. We must now devise a plan that will best protect our people, our kingdom and our way of life."

When he finished speaking, the silence in the room was deafening. Not even a breath could be heard, for all knew the gravity of the situation.

Jim sensed it was now his time to address the council, so he slowly stood up. "Fellow Deloresans, in life, many times we face obstacles that we would rather not face. Today, I would prefer that my lovely wife, Juliosa, was still by my side, but the reality is she is not. There is nothing I can do about that. And today, as Sir Traegan has so aptly explained, great danger approaches our kingdom, whether we desire it or not. So what are we to do?"

He sensed that all attention was firmly fixed on him, and that everyone in the room awaited the next words out of his mouth. "As Sir Traegan and I spoke last night of our predicament, I have decided that we need to send out our best sailors with our swiftest boats. We must try to find the other lands, which were separated from Eredia in the great earthquake, so that we can send for help from any surviving peoples. Our hope is that they will come to our aid. In the meantime, the rest of us will shore up our defenses, and prepare to meet our foe face to face in battle!"

The room erupted with praise as all cheered the king and his plan.

Jim, feeling more and more comfortable in his newly acquired position, raised the glass in front of him and said, "For Delores!"

At this, everyone resoundingly replied, "For Delores!"

Although Delores was the only kingdom in Eredia to possess mountains, their city was on the south side of them. The people of

Delores had to take their ships upriver on the mighty waters of the Lunaba and connect to other rivers to make it out to the vast Mergon Sea. The next day Traegan oversaw the preparations of the vessels. There were five ships chosen for this immense task, and each ship would take twenty of the bravest men of Delores with enough provisions for two weeks of travel. As well, each ship carried a dozen messenger pigeons, so that if they made contact with other lands, they could send word back to Delores of the news.

The preparations were finished quickly that day, for all knew the task and timeframe set before them. They had until the next full moon to procure help, *if* there was any help to be found. That night they all feasted in honor of the valiant sailors who volunteered for this mission of utmost importance. None of them knew if they would even return, none of them knew if they would be able to find the help their people needed, and, if they returned to Delores, none of them knew if they would find their people still alive. It was the most somber feast any of them ever attended in their lifetimes.

Very early the next morning, just as the sun crested in the west, all one hundred of the sailors said their goodbyes to their wives and children, and they boarded their assigned ships. The atmosphere was hard to describe, because it was so overwhelming for all. There was less than three weeks before the next full moon, and both the weight of despair and hope lay heavy on each Deloresan's heart that morning.

Chapter 8 - A Plea for Help

There was no time to waste. Jim knew that if they put all their hope in their ships finding the other lands, this was a very big gamble. And hoping they would *actually* find people in numbers enough to help them fight this evil alliance against King Fobe was an even greater risk. He was neither willing to cast those lots nor put all his chips on the table with that hand. They needed a backup plan, and he and Sir Traegan began work on it immediately.

The secondary plan was to shore up their defenses and also to provide a way of escape, at least for the women and children in the event that their plans utterly failed. With that, Jim ordered an escape tunnel to be dug through the heart of Delores Mountain. For on the other side of Delores Mountain lay a valley and a stream for his people to escape if necessary. He hoped they need not make use of this, but any prudent king would do the same. Hope for the best, yet plan for the worst.

He divided the remaining forces into two camps: those who were digging the tunnel and those who laid traps and ambushes for King Fobe and his menacing horde. It was unthinkable to the people of Delores that such evil could overtake their land in such a short period of time, but no matter what they thought, the reality completely contradicted their thoughts.

The Kingdom of Delores lay on the south side of the Mattagar Mountains, a vast range of divinely crafted crags and rocks, but to the south of Delores was the sprawling forest of Bendulum. And this forest was where Sir Traegan led half of the force to set up ambushes and traps. They set up booby traps and rigged several bridges along the path in order to cause the most devastation against Fobe's army. For Jim's army, this forest was certainly the choke point against his foe where he had the chance to inflict the maximum damage against them. Once they made it through Bendulum forest, there was nothing but a wide open valley and the Lunaba River, standing between them and Delores.

King Fobe was no fool, though, because he knew all this. He knew that his army would need to advance on King Jimban's lands through Bendulum forest, and they would certainly ambush them there. That is why he contrived several ways to combat those efforts in order to put his own army in a position to succeed over the Deloresans.

First, he certainly had no intentions of losing any of his *own* men in that forest, so he planned to have the soldiers from Thulda and Pampa spearhead their advance through the dense forest. This way, when the ambushes and traps sprang, the men from Caldan would not die first. This was a very sinister plot, but this was to be expected from King Fobe.

Second, Fobe hatched a plan to send two divisions of his soldiers by sea in order to navigate the waters of the Lunaba, which would place them right at the doorsteps of Delores, with half of Jim's army trapped in between. For whatever reason, neither Jim nor Traegan thought that

Fobe would send his men down the Lunaba River for a number of reasons. Number one, there are only so many men you can place on a river boat, especially one that is able to navigate those treacherous waters. Secondly, they thought that somehow, Fobe's armies may try to come *over* the Mattagar Mountains, ambushing them from behind and above, so that was what they prepared for.

Sir Laedo knew all the strengths and weaknesses of Delores, and he grew up navigating the waters of the Lunaba. He was all too willing to divulge what necessary information Fobe needed to win the battle. So, Fobe put Laedo in charge of leading the naval offense. That way, too, if Laedo died in the river, it would be no loss to Fobe. Laedo was simply a means to an end for him; he was the catalyst Fobe needed for total domination of the land of Eredia.

It would take Fobe's naval vessels two weeks to travel the sea and reach the confluence waters of the Lunaba, but it would only take one week for his army to make the march to Delores. With that knowledge, he planned a strategy so that their entire force would fall upon King Jimban all at once, hoping to overwhelm their defenses, for Fobe knew that would be the only chance they had of breaching the seemingly impenetrable mountain kingdom.

Jim's forces were hard at work tunneling through Delores. Not only were they on a tight deadline, but they needed to dig this tunnel in a manner that would also conceal the entryway from the enemy, if by chance they breached the city. They did not want the enemy to easily follow them through the tunnel and overtake them. The tunnel needed to provide the necessary time for them to evade and safely escape, or else it proved worthless.

The tunnel force broke into two groups so they could work night and day. The work on the tunnel never stopped. While one group slept, the other worked, and then they switched. This work was absolutely back-breaking and required a lot of strength and endurance. Nevertheless, the people of Delores, to Jim's delight, rose to the occasion. Their vigor and unity truly was an amazing sight to behold, and it almost baffled their king, for he had never witnessed such determination in the face of such impending doom.

During all the preparation, Jim barely slept, and he hardly ate. Neither of which was a good combination. He thought of Lauren and his family, and he wondered, "Will this be my last journey inward? Is this my final battle? I can't imagine I will survive this onslaught." He dearly hoped that Lauren was okay, and that nothing worse happened to her after he was hit by the bus. He could not imagine the thoughts that were running through her mind about him right now, but he wished with all his heart that he could tell her, in some way, how much he cared for her and missed her right at that moment.

Little did he know that Lauren, with some of his friends from college, were at the hospital with him, where he lay in a coma, and every free moment she had was spent right at his side, holding his hand in comfort. Lauren was a marvelous young lady full of knowledge and wisdom beyond her years, which initially caught Jim's attention. It certainly did not hurt that she was also very beautiful, like a sunrise in the Caribbean which perpetually repeats itself every moment of every day. Jim lay in the hospital, because he tried to stop her assailant. For this, she felt terrible, and she faithfully stayed by his side during this traumatic time.

Jim's mom and dad, along with members from their church, were all at the hospital as well. Anel and Brent took turns being at the hospital, while they kept John and Theresa abreast of the situation, since neither lived near Chicago any longer.

At the very moment that Jim hoped to convey his heart to Lauren, she was sitting by him holding his hand, and all of a sudden the words, "Lauren, I miss you," were clearly heard by her.

This stunned her because Jim still lay in a coma with all the hospital gadgetry hooked up to him to monitor what life still abided within him.

"Jim, Jim, are you okay?" Lauren almost shouted at him.

She tried to gently shake him and wake him. Anel was half-asleep when this happened, but when it happened she shot right up.

"Lauren, did he wake up?" she asked.

"I don't know. I was sitting here holding his hand, and all of the sudden I heard him say, 'Lauren, I miss you," Lauren explained. "He did not move or make any other sounds, so I don't know what to make of it."

Anel retrieved one of the nurses to check him out, but she found that he had not changed, for the good or the bad. They were back to patiently waiting and praying.

Jim had no clue any of this happened, and he certainly did not realize he was lying in a hospital in a comatose state. His last memory was that of colliding with the front of the city bus, but for now his present reality was that of war. He knew that if he did not succeed in his current reality, it would be the end of every reality for him. And he was not too keen on this idea.

The ships of Delores, after leaving the waters of the Lunaba, entered the great Mergon Sea. From there, they spread out as much as they could and bid each other farewell, knowing that for some, if not most, it would be the last time they saw each other. The crews headed out to the west, northwest, north, northeast and east. They hoped this would increase their chances of finding someone, *anyone* that may be willing to come to their aid. At that point, they were absolutely desperate. Yet even in their despair they remained full of hope.

The plights of these crews were all so different. The crews that set out to the east and northeast, unfortunately, met their end sooner than anyone hoped. An immense storm arose from the south as they travelled onward and after several hours of fighting for their very lives, the crew succumbed to the storm's overwhelming power and force. The bottom of Mergon Sea became their final resting place and with this catastrophe, the chances of the Deloresans finding help narrowed. This left only three ships to find help.

The crew to the north, after one week of sailing, discovered land. They were overly excited because they were not sure they would actually find land, let alone do it so quickly. At first sight, though, there were no signs of other people on this land, so they decided to navigate up one of the rivers to look. That decision proved fatal for their whole crew because after three days of exploring, the entire crew contracted a deadly disease from drinking some of the poisoned waters of that dreadful land. Three crews down now with only two left. Of course, none of the other crews knew any of that, and certainly neither did the people of Delores. That was probably best so that it did not compound their present despair.

The fate of the two remaining ships to the northwest and west was much better. In a strange twist of events, through some navigational error, both ships, after sailing for one and a half weeks, found the same land. The land of Furlham. However, each landed on opposite sides. And to their great astonishment, they found signs of life right away. Both crews, after convincing the locals that they indeed came in peace, asked to be taken to their king. The crew who sailed west was led upriver to the king's palace, and brought into his court. Just at that moment, the northwest crew docked at the river bank, and noticed the fellow Deloresan ship. They were absolutely dumbfounded.

They communicated to their Furlhaman guides that the ship at the dock was one of their own, and realized that both crews somehow found the same land. The Furlhaman soldiers lead the northwest crew into the king's court as well, and when they did, they found the west crew standing there before the king. When the northwest crew entered the court, the west crew, along with everyone else in the court, turned to look and they could not believe their eyes. Both crews rushed to greet one another. Even though there were forty foreign soldiers now in the king's court, there was no perceived threat to the king because they all were made to leave their weapons on their ships. They complied because as the saying goes, "desperate times call for desperate measures."

The king of the Furlhamans, King Storid, was a most gracious and welcoming king. He listened to their plight and plea, and decided to convene his military counsel the following day to decide what, if anything, they could do to help. That night they all feasted together because regardless of the doomful situation the Deloresans faced, it was still amazing that after a thousand years, people from other lands were still alive and able to discover each other. This was cause for great celebration. The Deloresans found it bittersweet, because they knew the great trouble facing their people back home. They hoped the night would not last long, so the counsel could convene soon.

The next morning, at first light, King Storid convened his military counsel. They listened to the plea of the Deloresans, as they explained the plot of King Fobe, and how he deceived the Thuldan and Pampan people, convincing them to take up arms against their people to conquer the whole of the island, despite having lived in peace and harmony for so many centuries. When they finished pleading for help, there was not a Furlhaman in the room that was not full of rage at the plot of Fobe.

They, too, had experienced a similar battle between their people and the other people of the land. Thankfully, though, they were able to assassinate the other king before a full war broke out, and the people decided to unify, making one people. But all the rage in the world would not help the Deloresans if the Furlhamans did not tangibly come to their aid.

The captain of the west crew seized upon their rage to passionately plead their cause further, "King Storid and all you honored people of the land of Furlhaman, hearing your story and how you faced a similar danger brings comfort to my ears. For you know as intimately as anyone that the danger we face is real, not a fairy tale. So, I ask you, will you help us? Will you fight alongside the Deloresans against this great tide of evil?"

At this, King Storid rose to his feet, and demanded an answer from his counsel, "What say you, people of Furlhaman? Will we fight?"

The air was choked thick with tension, because all knew the severity of the decision before the counsel. They knew that, if they did not go fight, the Deloresan people would certainly be wiped out, but they also knew that if they did go to their aid, many of their own people would certainly perish. What were they to do?

One by one, all six members of the counsel stood in approval, pledging their support from the different regions of Furlhaman. The Deloresans erupted in jubilant celebration, and there were hugs and joyful thanks all around. The captain of the west crew bowed in a show of gratitude towards the king and the war counsel for such a favorable decision.

The captain of the northwest crew then spoke up, "We must send word to our people immediately, and we must make haste to return to Eredia. There is no time to lose, for the next full moon will soon be upon us, and King Fobe's forces will be poised to attack."

King Storid agreed, and placed his leading military commander, General Corbin, in charge of their expeditionary force. Storid pledged a thousand men with forty ships, and they had only two days to prepare for their departure.

Meanwhile, both crews let loose four pigeons each with the news that they had, indeed, found one of the other lands, and they were bringing military aid. Their hope was that at least one of those pigeons made it back to Eredia and back to Delores to bring some measure of hope to their people. Now they prepared to make the long sail back, and thankfully the Furlhamans resupplied their ships with plenty of food and water for the return trip.

Back in Eredia, Traegan left one of his men in charge of the ambush preparations, and rode back to Delores to brief King Jimban on their progress. As he entered through the Great Gate, he saw two pigeons descending into the city, and his heart leapt for joy. Both the pigeons confirmed the amazing news: help was on the way. The entire city exploded with joy and hope. The news travelled fast to those digging the tunnels and to those in Bendulum forest. That night all Deloresans rejoiced with mirth and dancing, not knowing that Sir Laedo's naval force made its way up the eastern coast of Eredia to get to the Lunaba, and soon a force three times their own would invade their land, like locusts blanketing the countryside.

Chapter 9 - The Impending Battle

All the chess pieces moved into place on the board as planned. King Fobe and his land forces marched north on Delores. Traegan and his army were ready with their traps and ambushes in the Bendulum forest. King Jimban and the city were as ready as they could be with the defenses and the tunnel. Laedo and his naval forces approached the mouth of the Lunaba from the Mergon Sea. And the remaining two expeditionary ships returned with a large allied force of a thousand men in tow aboard forty ships. This was shaping up to be the battle of the ages.

Jim stood on the top of the king's tower, the tallest tower in Delores, looking out over his dominion, trying to mentally grasp everything that was rapidly unraveling before his very eyes. He was still trying to come to terms with the fact that he was going to war...again. "What am I doing? I am no warrior and I am certainly no king," he said to himself. "Why can't I ever defeat this enemy? Every time I come into this other world, I always fight against this masked man, yet I can never defeat him. I can't defeat him and he has never defeated me. Why?" Jim mused to himself. Little did he know that this battle would change his life forever in ways he never fathomed.

The plan called for Traegan and his men to deploy their attack on Fobe's army while they slowly moved through the forest, and then fall back to the city to make a defense. They already had word that their crews were coming with help, but they were not certain *exactly* when they would arrive. Not only that, they still had no clue about Laedo's naval force moving to ambush them by the river. Each force had each other ambushed; the problem was that one force knew it while the other did not.

The next full moon was in three days' time. Fobe was trying to give Laedo enough time to bring his two divisions around by the sea in order to fully ambush Traegan's men and cut them off, and he knew this was a gamble for his whole plan. It was a sadistic gamble he was willing to take. In his mind, even if he lost, he still won. That is always how it is with megalomaniacs.

With only one day until the full moon, Laedo's forces reached the mouth of the Lunaba, and begin their dangerous journey up the mighty river. Their goal was to make it halfway and set up camp for the night to await the full moon, and then move on Delores the following day just as Fobe ordered him. He was eager to complete his betrayal of King Jimban, and he knew his chance was now.

Unbeknownst to Laedo the allied forces reached the northwest coast of Eredia, and swiftly made their way to the mouth of the Lunaba. They wanted to waste no time returning to Delores, so, after setting up camp at the mouth of the river, they planned to set sail for the city at first light.

King Jimban and his force were not expecting Laedo's naval forces, and Laedo was not expecting the Furlhamans. In fact, he knew nothing of these people or that the Deloresans had even sent for help. As far as everyone on Eredia knew, there was *no help* to be found beyond the Mergon Sea. Unfortunately for him and King Fobe, they had no contingency in place for failure.

The next morning, as the first ray of sunlight peeked up from the west, the allied forces packed up and set sail up the Lunaba. They would reach Laedo's forces about mid-day and despite the fact that they outnumbered the allied naval forces two-to-one, their forces were surely in for a great surprise.

The allied forces sailed swiftly up the Lunaba with the northwest crew leading, and the north crew in the middle. Each ship was a guide for the ships that trailed behind them. From some distance away, they saw smoke from fires up ahead on the other side of a bend in the river, so they decided to pull off to the side of the river to send a scouting team to investigate.

Twenty minutes later, the scouting team returned with the dreadful news. The bad news was that they were outnumbered, but the good news was that they were *all on land*. Their ships were docked in the river, so the allied forces had the element of surprise. They decided to wait for cover of night, and hope that was not too late.

With the dark canopy set above and the fully lit moon to guide their ships on the water, the allied forces began their stealth attack on Laedo. Laedo's men were not set to head out for two more hours, so they were still unsuspecting. This played out perfectly into the allied forces hands. General Corbin, the commander of the Furlhaman forces, was very excited about this opportunity. He did not sail all this way to return home with a clean sword. Just think of him as a modern day U.S. Marine; always ready for battle!

As they approached them, the plan called for the first ship to take on the forces docked on the eastern side of the river, and the next ship to take on the western forces. Then each ship behind would duplicate that pattern. In that way, they would completely and evenly fall upon their enemy, dividing them up, ensuring a greater chance of success for the ambush.

Laedo's men did not even have watchmen posted, because, in their arrogance, they felt they had no need of them. This worked out well for the allied forces. As soon as the first ship turned towards the eastern shore and the second turned towards the western shore, every ship afterwards, in turn, replicated them, and then the flaming arrows flew up. General Corbin cried out, "Charrrrrgggee!" At this, every man quickly disembarked from the ships and charged the camps of the enemy. Laedo's men really had no clue what to do. There was mass chaos.

The allied forces, with the help of their flame-archers from the ships, moved swiftly from tent to tent putting their enemy to the sword, and Laedo's men were so confused that many of them ended up fighting against each other, aiding the allied forces, since their numbers were fewer to begin with.

As General Corbin and the Furlhamans routed Laedo's naval forces, King Fobe and his army of five thousand men began their march through the Bendulum forest. He ordered no torches to be lit along the march, so they would not make themselves easy targets. Although, marching in a forest at night under a full moon has the tendency to already do that.

Traegan's men lined the road entering the forest with tar, and their plan was to wait for enough of Fobe's men to enter the forest, and then light the hidden tar aflame, trapping many of them in a veritable tunnel of fire. They hoped this would take out several hundred men, but also slow their advance on the city.

King Fobe positioned himself at the middle of the entire column of soldiers. He figured he would lose about half of the army through the forest, but he counted on gaining two thousand men back, when Laedo's men arrived. Little did he know that Laedo's forces were struck down, just as his forces began their march.

They entered the forest, and, after ten minutes of row after row of soldiers entering the fire zone, Traegan's men let loose flaming arrows to hit along the road. As soon as the arrows hit the road, flames burst forth from the ground, like a dragon arising from the depths of Hades. The flames swallowed hundreds of these soldiers alive and sparked fear in the hearts of the rest of Fobe's army.

After an hour of fetching water from the nearby creek to quell the dragon's mouth and the flames died down enough, they cleared the burnt bodies off the road and proceeded to march forward. Each soldier carried a body length shield, because they expected arrows to be let loose all along the way. They were not disappointed.

The road through Bendulum forest was not extravagantly wide, yet it was no mere trail either. It allowed men to walk ten abreast, providing enough space for a large number of soldiers to move at a brisk pace. The Deloresans knew that if they could get Fobe's men to stop at different intervals, they would be more prone to attack. From end to end, the point through which the main road crossed through was only seven miles long. Long enough to inflict damage but not long enough to completely impede their movement forever.

Traegan's men were able to mostly see the columns of Fobe's army because of the bright moon light. It was nothing compared to the light of day, but it was certainly better than nothing. They used that light to their advantage and let their arrows fly as often as possible. The weak point on the enemy's armor at that point was their neck, the sides of their heads and the bottom portion of their legs. Those were the only exposed areas their large shields allowed for Traegan's men to take aim.

Many arrows bounced off their shields and helmets, but some were able to penetrate flesh, causing the soldier to flail on the ground, which exposed the soldiers to the rear and side of him. When that happened, the Deloresan archers were ruthlessly accurate, and took out eight to ten men per occurrence. That tactic slowed the march of the evil alliance, but it was definitely *not* grinding it to a halt, for the Caldan, Pampan and Thuldan soldiers also returned fire, striking some of the Deloresans. Soon, Fobe planned to unleash his own major counter attack against the guerilla fighters. In the meantime, Traegan's forest forces kept up the pressure.

Back at Laedo's camp, much of the enemy fled into the woods rather than be slaughtered, but many, if not most, were put to the sword. General Corbin captured Laedo, and brought him bound to the captains of the north and northwest crews. Some of the allied forces fell at the hands of the enemy as well, but they were far and few between. Once they finished the assault, they took what weapons and provisions were around, so as to not leave the remaining enemy soldiers who were hiding in the woods with any supplies. They set their vessels on fire, and continued their voyage up the Lunaba to Delores.

They attacked the enemy at the halfway point to the city, so they had several more hours of sailing upriver to reach the final destination. Thankfully, they had a very good tailwind to move them along at a rapid pace. Even though there was a full bright moon beaming down upon them and even though they were guided by the Deloresans, still some of the Furlhaman ships succumbed to the mighty waters of the river. Out of the forty ships they sent, thirty two survived the entire trip. Lunaba was beautiful and mighty, but forgiving she was not. It was sad for the men to have crossed such a great distance only to meet their final fate so close to the great city they swore to protect.

Just before dawn rose from her sleep, the allied forces arrived beneath the cover of the Lunaba Bridge. The captains of the expeditionary crews, along with General Corbin, disembarked from their vessels, taking Laedo with them to approach the city. At a safe distance, they called to the gate guards to tell them who they were and to not shoot. The guards were completely astonished, and quickly sent word to King Jimban. Jim had been at the peak of his tower, watching for any signs from Traegan's men or from the guards in the mountains. He still did not know if some of Fobe's men would try to ambush them from the protection of the crags.

But as soon as Jim received word that his expeditionary forces returned, he nearly flew down the stairs of his tower, mounted his horse and swiftly road to the front gate. The guards already confirmed it was their men, and brought them inside. When Jim arrived, his captains presented both General Corbin and Sir Laedo to him, and told him of the remaining forces still docked down at the river.

He could hardly believe his ears, because it seemed almost impossible for his forces to find the other lands, let alone come back with such a large contingent of allied forces to help them as well. On top of that he could not believe that he and Traegan naively left their defenses open to a naval attack by Fobe, but was so thankful that his men, along with the Furlhamans routed them in their surprise attack. With the crushing of Laedo's forces and the sudden appearance of an allied force of over a thousand men, it seemed as if they now stood a chance to defeat King Fobe. His mind swirled with hope, when shortly before it was only clouded with despair.

Jim ordered Laedo to be sent to the dungeon and locked up. When the battle was over, he planned to try him on charges of high treason. Then he had General Corbin bring his men into the city, so that they could be cared for and take some much needed rest. They needed to preserve their strength for tomorrow's battle. The entire city was over-elated at the news and as the morning rays of the sun slowly appeared, their optimism overflowed.

Traegan and his men, on the other hand, were not so optimistic. It seemed that no matter what they threw at King Fobe's forces, like the little engine that could, he refilled their ranks and continued their push onward. At every hour, he sent word to Jim by a runner to keep him informed of their defensive efforts, and to alert him as to how much time they had before the alliance burst forth from the wooded cover onto the open valley that lay before Delores.

As Jim sent his runner to the king, a new runner returned and with him, he brought news of the Furlhaman's allied forces and Laedo's subsequent defeat on the Lunaba. This greatly invigorated Traegan and his men, and their spirits and courage rose to the heavens, as an eagle soaring atop the winds.

With the news, came instructions from King Jimban for Traegan to cease the attack and regroup with the city as soon as possible. Fobe's army only had two more miles to go until they reached the open valley, so Traegan thought it best to have his men fall back now and retreat. At this, he had one of his captains sound the retreat horn, and all his men knew the plan.

Unknown to Sir Traegan, though, Fobe brought with his army a host of ferociously trained war-wolves. Each of Fobe's men, before they began their march on Delores, was sprayed with a scent that was an indicator to the wolves that they were not to attack them. Instead, they were trained to pursue their enemies.

Just as Traegan and his men ceased their attack and retreated, Fobe released nearly a hundred wolves to hunt down the hidden soldiers. With nearly two miles between them and their horses, the wolves had the upper hand. That was the counter-attack Fobe had up his sleeve, and waited for at the perfect opportunity. Not only was he evil, his timing was impeccable as well.

The Deloresan soldiers heard the howls of the wolf hoards pursuing them, and they retreated as fast as they could. But the reality was that they had two legs while the creatures pursuing them had four. That meant they were covering twice the space in half the time as the Deloresans. Math was not on their side at the moment.

All the men attempted to rally together and make haste for a nearby creek bed. This way, they could still retreat at a quick pace all the while defending themselves as best as possible against such a fierce force. This did not work out as planned, and their forces were split in two. One made it to the creek bed on the east side of the road, while the other made it to a trail on the west side of the road. This left the main road wide open, and Fobe's men advanced unabated. Little did they know, Traegan's men still had a few hidden tricks up their sleeves before Fobe's men exited the forest.

As the creek bed group moved along, they hurriedly jogged. The front men ran towards the rear shooting at any wolves that came near their group, and then they fell back in line. They repeated this tactic until they reached the edge of the forest, where they could mount their horses and outpace the wolves. This strategy proved very effective, because only a few of their men fell to the salivating mouths of those treacherous beasts.

The trail group was not so fortunate. Their whole group did not have as much cover as their counterparts, and their defense was to keep running as fast as they could and strike at any wolves that came near them. The only thing that saved *some* of their group from being completely overrun was the fact that each man that was attacked by the wolves drew several wolves away as they feasted on the body. This was literally survival of the fittest, and Darwin would be proud.

The men of the trail made it to their horses first, because their pace was much quicker than the creek group. They quickly mounted their steeds, and made like the wind towards Delores without looking back. Several minutes later, the creek group made it to their horses, and followed suit toward the city as well. All that stood between Fobe's army and Delores now was less than two miles of a booby-trapped road and an open valley.

The sun had full command of the morning by this point, so the alliance could travel at full pace. The sound of battle would soon resound in the Deloresan valley as the Mattagar Mountains looked on, no longer able to guard their treasured people.

King Fobe and his deceived alliance continued their determined march through Bendulum forest, and they thought the worst of the forest was behind them. Yet some retribution awaited them. Traegan and his men had hollowed out a fifty yard portion of the road, and planted a plethora of spikes in the dirt. Then, they built a covering for the road out of logs and cloth, covering it with dirt to disguise its frailty. The trap was set, and once enough weight pressed upon it, the spikes gleefully awaited to receive their gifts of flesh.

As the alliance made their way down a small hill and climbed the other side, the weight of the men caused the trap to open its mouth and receive the unsuspecting men. Almost every man who fell into the pit instantly died, but a few were merely wounded. Nevertheless, they were left to their own devices as the ranks behind walked around the pit and marched onward. Nearly two hundred men perished with this one trap, thus dwindling Fobe's numbers even further. Mind you, he still did not know that Laedo and his naval forces were summarily crushed; he still thought he would soon emerge from the forest with Traegan's men caught in between. He was in for a surprise, although he will not find this one very amusing.

By the time the alliance made it around the pit and out onto the plains of Delores valley, Traegan and his nearly four hundred horsemen made it back to the protection of the city. They performed superbly at holding up the enemy's forces, and inflicted great casualties upon them as well. All told, they were able to eliminate nearly two thousand men through the night, which is what Fobe planned for. However, he had not planned to have his naval force of two thousand to be fully thrashed by an unsuspecting ambush.

When Traegan entered Delores, he could not believe what he saw - the two crews who had returned with nearly a thousand men from Furlhaman, who answered the call to aid their people. Jim was very glad to have Traegan back because he knew that he was indispensable to their entire battle against Fobe. Even though, in his present reality, Jim was the king and older than he, he still drew comfort by having him near.

But in the end, Jim knew it was he, not Traegan, who had to lead the allied forces into battle. With this weighing heavily upon his mind, his thoughts turned toward Lauren and his family, and he dearly missed them. He wished he was there with them to laugh and find comfort, but they were nowhere to be found. He knew that his only way back to them was through the ravages of this imminent battle.

Jim brought Traegan, along with General Corbin, with their whole war counsel together to decide the best course of action against the great army at their door. Several options were on the table. First, they could all exit through the secret tunnel that was made over these past few weeks. Second, their people could quickly make their way onto ships and leave their cherished city behind to live (and fight) another day. Or, as Sir Traegan and General Corbin advocated, they could ride out and meet the enemy head on in the Delores Valley.

Taking into account the amount of casualties inflicted on the enemy by Traegan's men in the Bendulum forest and General Corbin's men along the banks of the Lunaba, the counsel figured that their forces were now nearly equal to those of Fobe's. With that knowledge, they voted to ride out against the enemy, but they would not do so until the following day. Traegan and his men, along with General Corbin's soldiers, needed some rest and refreshment before charging headlong back into battle.

Finally, like a champagne bottle cork, King Fobe's alliance burst forth from the shadowed road of the Bendulum forest, and out onto the lighted plains of Delores Valley. The beautiful valley with the city of Delores set amongst the Mattagar Mountains was certainly an imposing sight to behold for the alliance. Laedo had briefed them of the city's enormity and grandeur, but seeing it with their own eyes was completely different than merely hearing a verbal description of something that sublime.

As imposing as this sight was to them, not seeing Laedo and his forces at the Lunaba River was far more chilling to the leaders of the Pampans and Thuldans, and they quickly made their objections known to Fobe.

"King Fobe, you said that Laedo and his men would be here, and they are not. We no longer possess the upper hand, and would you require us to continue our attack against this impenetrable fortress with such great mountains watching over it?"

Despite the objections from the leaders of the Pampans and Thuldans, Fobe knew that the majority of the men who were still alive were the soldiers from Calda, which was his plan all along, so, after affirming his desire to still press the attack, he also made a decree that any soldier caught trying to escape the battle was to be executed immediately. Fobe's treachery, once hidden just like his masked face, was now fully seen.

With that, the evil alliance set up camp in the Delores Valley, and made preparations for their attack the following day. Their preemptive assault on the city would never materialize, however, because the Deloresans already voted to attack them. Tomorrow, at first light, that would become very evident.

Chapter 10 - Expecting the Unexpected

That night, despite his best efforts and despite the fact that the city was well guarded, Jim could not sleep a wink. Could you? Surely not. In just a few hours, the fate of his entire life would be determined by the outcome of just one battle that may or may not actually be real, since this incessant battle against fear was always in his mind. Was it not? The battle in his mind raged through the whole of the night. Phobophobia threatened to subdue him before the skirmish ever took place.

Finally, Jim got out of his bed and sat down in one of the chairs before his fireplace, and, before he knew it, he had a pipe in one hand as he contemplated his entire life and the unending fight against his fear. He reminisced on all his battles and all the places he had travelled to, but he also remembered all the havoc he wreaked on his relationships with friends and family alike. He desired greatly for this internal war to finally be over. That wish would soon be granted, but not in a way he hoped.

As he gazed upon the fire, there was a knock at the door. "Enter," Jim said.

At this, Traegan entered his room, and this brought a measure of peace to Jim's soul at the moment. "Good morning, Your Majesty. Have you been able to sleep," he inquired?

"No more than you have, I see," Jim responded.

Traegan sat in the chair opposite Jim.

Then he said in a very serious manner, "I am very thankful the Giver granted our vessels favor with finding the Furlhamans and for sending them to our aid. Hope has come when we thought that it had all but vanished."

Jim agreed with him, "You are very right, Traegan. Very right. We are most fortunate indeed."

"Your Majesty, even with the reinforcements from Furlhaman, do you believe that we will be able to defeat Fobe and his alliance?" he asked Jim.

Jim took his time before answering, because he could sense that Traegan was wrestling with some doubts, just as he was. After a few moments, he responded, "I cannot, in good conscience, believe that the Giver has brought so many men to our aid from so distant a land as to not allow our victory this day." He paused and then continued, "However, even if we win the battle, many of us will surely perish. No man is guaranteed breath for more than the day he presently faces."

"A very wise insight, Your Majesty. Thank you for helping me steady my anxieties," Traegan said. "It's just that, when we were being chased by those wolves, I thought for sure my time to meet the Giver had come and this thought terrified me more than any thought about the menacing foe which now stands before us."

Jim took in and processed everything he heard, and said, "I understand how you feel. The thing about it, though, is that every man will someday face the Giver. How we do so, however, is up to us." Jim stood to his feet, walked towards Traegan, and put his hand on his shoulder to comfort him. "Everything will be alright, Traegan. You are my fiercest and bravest warrior. Be at peace." Traegan rose to embrace his king.

"Now, let us ready ourselves for battle. We must see to our men and our people. They, too, must be strengthened and encouraged before any of us steps outside the protecting walls of this beloved city." And with that, Jim led Traegan out, so they could try and eat some food before donning their armor.

As Jim stepped outside of his fortress, he took in the breathtaking view of the clear dark sky with the bright, full moon smiling down upon him as if it were the Giver, himself, showing his approval of Jim and the fate of his people. The stars in the dark expanse twinkled and danced in exuberant freedom, for there was nothing for them to fear. How Jim envied them at that very moment.

While he took in the beautiful vista, General Corbin approached him, and Jim noticed that he was already suited for battle. That impressed Jim, but it quickly reminded him that battle was soon.

"Good morning, King Jimban. It is a fine day to crush our enemies," Corbin said.

Jim took note of Corbin's resounding assurance, as if he knew something that he did not. "Indeed it is, General Corbin. Indeed it is," Jim responded. "Have your men been well taken care by our people?"

Corbin answered, "Most graciously, Your Majesty."

"Very good. We cannot express in any known tongue the level of gratitude in our hearts for the aid that you and your people have brought to us. It is beyond words. So, please accept my simple, 'thank you,' for the time being," Jim said with tears welling up in his eyes.

Corbin grasped his right arm and said, "You are most welcome, Your Majesty!"

After checking on his men and the status of the city as a whole, Jim returned to his castle to try and eat something to garner strength for the battle and afterwards, he, with the help of his servants, put his battle armor on. When he was all suited up, they brought a mirror before him, and, when Jim saw himself, he almost fainted. He did not recognize the man in the mirror, and could not believe for one second it was him. For the man he saw was much older than he knew himself to be, and he looked commandingly impressive. Truth be told, he looked like a king.

Dawn soon approached and within a few hours, the first rays of the sun's morning light would pierce the skies around them, signaling the time to advance against the enemy before their very gate. It was not a battle the Deloresans asked for, but it was one they now stood ready to fight. King Jimban ordered that if the battle turned against the Deloresans, all the women and children were to make their way into the secret tunnel, and only a handful of young guards were to be left behind to watch after the city and the prisoners. As well, if the battle went south, they were ordered to help evacuate the city through the tunnel, and see to the safety of the women and children, hoping that Fobe's forces were unable to follow them.

The alliance camp stirred about. They did not know for certain if the Deloresans would come out to face them quickly, or if they would have to keep the city under siege for many weeks before they chose to face them. Either way, they were not going to be caught off guard; they were already more undermanned than planned. Even with the setback, however, their numbers were still in good shape.

Just as King Fobe was putting his armor on that morning, messengers arrived to share the news about Laedo's defeat. It was the soldiers who hid in the forest along the Lunaba. They made the trek across land to the valley and when they arrived, they filled Fobe in on all the details of the surprise ambush. As well, he learned that the Deloresans had found aid from people unknown to them. He was furious, to say the least, now knowing for sure that his reinforcements were not coming. Well, at least not all of them were coming; over three hundred men were able to escape into the woods and make it to the camp. His obstinate will still prevailed, though, and he gave orders that the alliance would remain there despite the defeat of the naval forces. He seemed bent on his own destruction.

Their first move, he decided, would be to ravage the kingdom's meadow, on the north side of the Lunaba, where all their fruits and vegetables grew. He figured that if they took away their food quickly, then they would be more apt to either give in to his demands or fight them in battle. His demented mind preferred the latter. Fobe would not send all his forces to accomplish this task. No, he was very cunning. He planned to send just enough to entice the enemy, to use them as bait to lure them into armed conflict.

Two hundred horsemen were ordered to set out for the mission. The sun had not risen yet; it was still pre-dawn. The alliance soldiers took off on their horses, and approached the Lunaba Bridge cautiously, not knowing if the Deloresans set any more traps, just as they did in the forest. None of these guys desired to meet a similar fate as their comrades had. Finally, they crossed over the bridge. The kingdom of Delores possessed such stunning beauty that the enemy had a hard time taking their eyes off of it. Even as they crossed over the Lunaba they seemed mesmerized by its grandeur. Despite the city's alluring affect, the men had orders to follow, and they definitely did not want to disobey Fobe.

Inside the city, the tower guards alerted King Jimban of the oncoming soldiers and he, in turn, ordered the entire army to quickly finish preparing for battle. The alliance soldiers started with the rows nearest the city and worked backwards, all the while keeping an eye out for Deloresan archers or soldiers. They were prepared, at any given moment, to make haste and retreat to their camp if they needed to. Their mission was to entice the enemy, not be captured by them.

Jim met with Traegan and General Corbin before all their men set out. "Sir Traegan, General Corbin, are all your men ready for battle?" he asked.

Traegan answered first, "They are, Your Majesty. They are ready to give their very lives for our people."

Then General Corbin said, "We, too, are ready, Your Majesty. The Furlhamans are not of this land but nevertheless, we stand ready to give our lives in defense of it."

And with that, the three leaders devised the best strategy to take on Fobe.

Their forces would, after crossing the Lunaba, spread out into three groups. King Jimban would lead the center group. Sir Traegan would lead the left flank, and General Corbin would lead his men on the right flank. Their hope was to force them back into the forest. At that point, they could set it on fire, and let the flames do the rest.

Fobe's men were all ready to exact some revenge for all the men they lost the previous night on their trek through the Bendulum forest. They would not be easily conquered by the Deloresans, and the battle was shaping up to be a fierce one. If the alliance won, they would rule the entire land of Eredia and now that they knew of people from other lands, they would most certainly set out to conquer them as well. If the Deloresans did not prevail, their entire way of life would vanish without a trace, and their people would be wiped out. Their entire destiny hinged on this battle. Today was their *D-Day*.

The alliance horsemen ravaged through the meadow of Deloresans cutting down trees, ripping out fruits and vegetables and gardens that were meticulous kept for hundreds of years. The tower guards looked on in horror at this travesty but for the present, there was nothing to be done. Not yet.

Just as the alliance minions were finishing up their mission, the Great Gate began to open, and they took notice. Quickly, the men mounted their horses, and rode as fast as they ever had. The men of Delores came riding and marching out of the city. They were not in a hurry. This battle would be fought on their terms, not the enemy's. King Jimban led the army and as they passed through the meadow, anger swelled within their hearts, for the enemy savages had wrought such destruction on their livelihood.

As they crossed the Lunaba Bridge, King Fobe's forces made ready for battle, and assembled into their groups. They, too, were positioned into three groups to represent the tripartite alliance between the Caldans, Pampans and Thuldans. The Delores Valley was a beautiful open plain with such a colorful blanket of green grass, but soon such beauty would be drenched in red, for that was the color of war. Red, always red.

Fobe, being the conniving devil he was, took the three hundred men who had survived the naval battle by escaping into the forest. He had them split up and hide in the forest. Their job was to ride around the flanks of the enemy by way of the forest and at the right time, attack the enemy from behind. That was their vulnerability, their weak spot, because the Deloresans would not be expecting an attack from their rear, since they just came from the city. And no other army would expect it either.

As Jim lead the allied forces onto the plain of Delores Valley, his mind wandered off to Lauren and his family, and it reminded him of when he was running through the jungle with Chewalahs, during one of his first inward travels. Then, just as now, he was fully experiencing the situation he was in, but he could also vividly see and understand his real life. It was like he was living two lives simultaneously, if such a thing could be imagined.

He sincerely hoped that Lauren and his family were well, and he really hoped that he would make it out of this battle alive. As his horse marched along, he pondered all the events that led up to this great battle, from his walk with Lauren, to her being robbed, to him being struck by the bus, to the betrayal by Sir Laedo, to the expeditionary force returning with aid, and now facing this grandiose and formidable foe outside of a kingdom, of which he was king. All of it was too mind-boggling to comprehend. But, comprehend it or not, the battle was not only Jim's to face; it was his to *lead*.

The allied forces spread out into their three groups as planned, and now the allied forces were set face to face with the alliance forces, ready to battle for the life of the Delores people and the future of the land of Eredia. The two forces were almost equally numbered against one another. I say, "almost," because there were three hundred alliance men lurking in the woods. Everyone involved knew the gravity of this battle. All felt its weight.

The sun rose in the west and shined upon the valley, upon the Mattagar Mountains and especially upon the city of Delores. The few guards that remained in the city, along with the women and children, looked on with such angst, not knowing if their army would prevail. Even if they prevailed, they knew that many of their loved ones would perish in the fight, sacrificing their lives for their liberation. In any case, those inside the city were prepared to make flight, if the worse should come.

The smell of sweat and metal and horses wafted through the air in the Delores valley. Vultures circled above, awaiting their feast, even as some already feasted on those slain in the forest, squabbling over whatever flesh the wolves left behind. The horses were eager to charge, while the men hesitated because even in defense of your very life, no one truly desires to die.

The Trumpeter stood next to Jim and when the tension could mount no more, he ordered him to sound the call to charge. At the blast of the trumpet, both armies, with shouts and swords raised, leapt towards one another, like the positive and negative sides of magnets, and very soon they would meet each other in a most terrible collision.

Jim, Traegan, and Corbin were all on horseback, along with some other men, so their job was to hold the line, and not get too far in front of their men. At a certain point, though, Jim's men would take the lead, so that they pierced the lines of the enemy like a hunter's arrow entering the side of a deer in the forest. From the vulture's point of view, however, it just looked like a bunch of ants squabbling over dirt. No matter to them - they just licked their lips, if vultures even have them.

Within just a few minutes from the trumpeter's blast, the two opposing forces collided, and the sound of battle echoed through the valley, eerily ricocheting off the mountains behind them. The fighting was fierce, and Jim proudly led his men in combat. For the most part, the Deloresans seemed to be thrashing the alliance and both Traegan's and Corbin's groups were beginning to encircle them. Both sides, however, were losing men left and right.

After twenty minutes of vicious combat and when the battle seemed to be favoring the Deloresans, King Fobe noticed that they drew the allied forces far enough away from the Lunaba Bridge and the rear edge of the forest, where he had three hundred horsemen poised to attack from behind. At that moment, Fobe had his trumpeter sound the blast and when the horsemen in the forest heard it, they knew that was their signal to ride out and attack.

The blast threw the allied forces into confusion, because they did not know what it meant. At first, they thought the enemy decided to retreat. As he fought against the enemy, Jim looked around, only to see the devastating sight - the horsemen attacking his army from the rear. His body went completely numb, because he knew they been utterly duped by Fobe. As he looked upon the horsemen, someone struck his horse with a spear, killing it and sending Jim and his horse toppling over, with the horse landing on him.

At that very moment, Lauren slept in a chair in his hospital room and when the horse landed on him, he let out a very loud gasp of air, which startled her from her sleep. She ran over to check on him, but still no response came. She quickly retrieved a nurse, explaining to her what happened and when the nurse checked him over, she found that he was okay. However, if they would have lifted his gown to examine his body, they would have found his chest and ribs full of deep bruises. Thankfully, they did not.

With the infusion of the horsemen, Fobe and his army quickly turned the tide of the battle and soon after Jim was brought down from his horse, both Traegan and General Corbin were also brought down and captured. The fight raged on until almost all the Deloresan men were struck down by sword, spear or arrow. The people inside the city of Delores looked on in horror as their forces were brought to ruin. At that sight, the orders to abandon the city through the secret tunnel were given by the chief guard, and all the women and children, along with the guards, did so as quickly as possible, for they knew it would not be long before the alliance marched upon the city.

As the fighting came to an end, everyone hunted for King Jimban and finally one of the Caldan soldiers found him pinned underneath his horse. He was not dead, just knocked unconscious from the fall.

King Fobe, with his masked face, walked over and stood over him, and let out a most evil laugh. "Now, all of Eredia is mine. And now, King Jimban, you are mine! Get him out from under that horse, and tie him up with the other prisoners."

The vultures wasted no time supping on the bodies of the dead. And that night, the alliance forces, along with the wolves of the forest, would feast as well. King Fobe ordered all the prisoners to be bound to one another, so that they could march upon the city. He knew that the Deloresans were crafty, so they cautiously approached the front gate, not wanting to lose any more men to some silly trap. But there was no trap to greet them. Instead, there was an empty city.

King Fobe and his goons entered through the Great Gate, and wasted no time searching through every part of it. Although they found much loot and plunder, there was no *person* to be found. The city was a veritable ghost town. That did not stop the alliance men from taking up residence in the homes. That night would be one of feasting and gloating over their enemies. They were now the rulers of the whole land of Eredia, and Fobe decided to make Delores the new epicenter of his rule. He started by sending King Jimban to the dungeon, along with the other prisoners, and taking up residence in his castle.

Jim was conscious, but I dare say he was not altogether there. He was violently knocked over in battle, and then a very large animal rolled upon him. His body groaned in immense pain, and he still was unable to process any coherent thoughts. He and Sir Traegan, along with

General Corbin were all thrown into the same dungeon cell, which happened to be right next to Sir Laedo's cell. Once they were thrown into the cell, Jim passed out from the pain, and, while he lay there, he dreamed of Lauren.

He even cried out for her, "Lauren, Lauren. Noooooo!"

Traegan and General Corbin were beside themselves as to who he was shouting for, but, nonetheless, they let him be.

All of the Deloresan men were beside themselves. The despair was so tangible, so real to them that they tasted it in their mouths, whether they wished to or not. Most of the men sat in their cells and wept. They wept for the slain. They wept for their king. They wept for Delores. But most of all they wept for their families, for their wives and children. They knew not whether they made it safely through the secret tunnel and if so, how far were they able to get. It was imperative they put as much distance between themselves and the rear side of Delores Mountain.

While the Deloresan men wept, the alliance, the champions of the day, prepared their feast. Chickens, ducks, pigs, fish, fruits, vegetables, and more wine than the waters of the Lunaba would be on the menu that evening. The sounds and smells of victory would be heard and smelled through the whole the city that night. King Fobe delighted greatly at the apex of his wicked plan, and his evil mind (and heart) rejoiced jubilantly that everything went just the way he hoped. Now, he was no longer merely the king of Caldan; he was now the Emperor of Eredia, and tonight the men of the alliance were to crown him as such. By now, the men of Thulda and Pampa realized that was his plan all along, and he used them to manifest it. But it was too late, for they were caught in the very web they helped spin. As the saying goes, hindsight is always twenty-twenty.

The women and children of Delores, along with the few remaining guards, made it safely through the tunnel, and they were making their way to the Mergon Sea. On the north side of Delores Mountain, there was another river. It was nothing compared to the mighty Lunaba, but nevertheless, it, too, was a beautiful river to behold. That river was called the Mattagar River, named for the very mountains through which it wound all the way to the sea. The plan called for them to follow the Mattagar River to the Mergon Sea. There were caves near the coast in which they could take refuge, and the sea would provide the food and the river the water. At least they would find protection and sustenance. For how long, though, no one knew.

Night settled in and the feasting was on full display in Delores. The sounds of the celebration echoed through the halls of the dungeon prison, and it only made the defeat for the men of Delores more unbearable. For they knew that those rascals were feasting in their own houses, devouring their own food and wine, all of which they worked so hard with their own two hands to produce. The only solace for them at the present moment came from the fact that their women and children were long gone. Had they not been, their defeat would have been compounded exponentially.

Traegan, although he was wounded in battle, was still alert, and he had his full wits about him. He knew that King Fobe would come to torture them tomorrow to get them to disclose where their women and children were hiding. He knew they needed to, somehow attempt to escape in the early morning, when the alliance men were still passed out from their previous night's celebration.

The dungeon guards made Fobe aware that Sir Laedo was also locked up, and they informed him that Laedo was captured during the ambush on the Lunaba. At that news, all the men expected him to free Laedo, but instead he said, "Sir Laedo failed me. When we came out of the forest, he was nowhere to be found. Was he? He should not have failed me. Now he will rot in that dungeon with the rest of the prisoners. And let that be a lesson to all of you. Do not fail me!"

Everyone in his presence was stunned at the emperor's command. They put in the hand of Fobe the cup of tyranny, and he planned to drink it down to the last of its dregs.

The guards returned and alerted Laedo of the emperor's command and at that news, it was his turn to weep. Not only had he betrayed the people of Delores, he was now captive in the dungeon of those very same people. Some call that karma, while others simply say that he was reaping what he sowed. No matter how you skin the cat in that circumstance, he was in an awful spot for sure.

Fobe assigned some of the remaining Thuldan and Pampan men to guard the prisoners, so that all of his men could dine and celebrate with him. Sometime later, Traegan overheard some of the guards talking. "King Fobe and the Caldans are up there feasting, while we are down here with nothing but scraps to eat. He used our people. He tricked us, and now he is our ruler."

When Traegan heard those words, he knew this was the opportunity they needed. "Pssst, Psst," he signaled for the guards to come near him.

The four guards walked down to his cell, "What do you want?"

Traegan replied, "Well, from what I heard you all say, it sounds like King Fobe really put one over on your people."

One of the guards shot back, "Says the man locked in his own dungeon."

"Quite right, ole boy. But here's the thing. If you help us escape from this dungeon, we will help you all escape from Fobe. He won't even know where you went," Traegan said, trying desperately to convince them of his plan.

As the guards mulled it over, Sir Laedo spoke up, "You men should listen to Sir Traegan. He is right. If you stay here, Fobe will only make you all his slaves. That was his plan all along, to make his own people rule over everyone. I am sorry I helped him do it, but at least you can save yourselves. You would be fools not to!"

At his persuasion, the guards accepted Traegan's deal. He then explained to them that once all the feasters passed out, early in the morning, they could open their cells and they would make their way to the secret tunnel. However, he did not disclose its location to them. He did this for two reasons: firstly, he did not want them to make use of it without setting them free, and secondly, if he told them the location, it would have frightened them out of the deal for sure.

Jim still lay in an unconscious state for several hours but at some point after midnight, he began to wake up.

"I am thirsty," he said. Traegan had some water brought over by the guards. He sipped on it, and afterwards, Traegan and Corbin gingerly helped him sit up against the wall.

"Where are we?" Jim asked, as his head dizzily buzzed.

"Your Majesty, we are in our own dungeon...in Delores" Traegan sheepishly told him.

"So then, we lost the battle?" Jim further questioned. That seemed more of a rhetorical question, so neither Traegan nor the General answered him.

After a few moments of silence, Traegan spoke up with controlled excitement, and explained to Jim the plan he hatched to get them all to safety. Jim sat there, listening to his plan, but all he could think about was the fact that he would be trapped in this world indefinitely. "What have I done? I knew this battle with fear would be my downfall. In all my other battles, I was always able to somehow escape. Not this time, Jim L'Beau. Not this time."

In his mind, he bemoaned his current state and when Traegan finished speaking, he asked Jim, "How does that sound?"

Jim had no clue what Traegan really said, so he simply said, "Sure."

Traegan and Corbin took that as an affirmative. That was it. In a few hours' time, before the sun rose again, they would escape. But would they succeed?

Chapter 11 - Internality Revealed

It was still a full moon that night, and it hung in the dark night sky like a beautiful family portrait perfectly mounted above a welcoming fireplace. The feasting and music ceased for several hours, so that was the guards' cue to release the prisoners. As the guards opened the cell doors, they skipped over Laedo's cell, determined to leave him rotting there, since he helped Fobe ascend to tyranny. However, when Traegan noticed that, he ordered the guards to release him as well.

"No one in this dungeon deserves to stay, no matter what they have done. We must all escape the clutches of this mad man."

At that, the guards released him, and Laedo embraced Traegan and thanked him for his kindness.

General Corbin helped Jim walk, because he could not stand on his own just yet. When Laedo saw this, he took up Jim's other side. It was an awkward moment, helping carry the man who was wounded because of your betrayal. Jim needed all the help he could to walk, so he raised no objections. With over a hundred men in tow, Traegan led the way. He was determined to get his king and his people to safety, even if it meant sacrificing his own life, which he was duly prepared to do. Hopefully, he would not have to.

Now came the tricky part of the escape, for it called for them to sneak into the king's court, where all the feasting took place the night before and where many soldiers were passed out asleep on the tables and the floor. The tunnel was dug behind the main fireplace in the court. I know you think that is madness, and it is! Nevermind, though, because right now, it was their only chance of escape. But then you may wonder, "Why don't they just go out the front gate?" Well, Fobe is no fool. He had his own Caldan men, not the Thuldans or Pampans, guard the front gate, so that no one would escape. Do you now better understand the precarious situation Jim and the captured Deloresans were in? Good.

The men stealthily made their way to the castle, and crept into the king's court. All of the men were passed out, and most, if not all, of them were snoring like a herd of snorting hogs. Let us not even mention the smell that filled the room, for it would turn even the strongest of stomachs. Traegan, along with five other men, snuck into the king's court and once they pulled the fireplace out enough to get the men through, they signaled for the men to begin trickling in, six at a time. It was not a very fast process, but it was the quietest one. Traegan and two other men stood guard to make sure that everyone safely made it into the tunnel before they went in themselves.

Everything was working just as planned, until two men, who were carrying a wounded man tripped on one of the Caldan's shields. The sound was that of a very large gong being rung at the start of a Japanese sumo match, but this match would be much worse. Many of the Caldans in the court sprung to their feet and just as the last of the prisoners made it into the tunnel, they rushed towards the fireplace. Traegan ordered the last two men to close the entrance. He then quickly grabbed a sword, and valiantly defended his escaping comrades. He was able to slay several of the Caldans before being mortally subdued himself.

With flight of feet, the escaping prisoners ran with what strength they could muster. Even though he was being helped along by two grown men, Jim still found it difficult to breathe. Jim knew that even though they narrowly escaped, since the Caldans found them out, it would not be long before they figured out how to open the fireplace themselves. They needed to put as much distance between them and their pursuers as possible.

Jim looked at the river, and had an idea.

"We need to make for the river. We need to swim downstream. The river will take us much further along than our feet will, especially since some of us cannot walk," he told his men.

There were logs near the river's bank, so they all grabbed onto some and put into the river. By the time the Caldans alerted Fobe of the escape and were able to gain access to the tunnel, Jim and his men were already around the first bend and out of sight. The river carried them along very quickly, but being that the Mattagar River is a mountain river, it was extremely cold. The men could ride its waves for only so long before they needed to leave its speedy currents, because the very water that was helping them began to drain them of their life, sucking the heat from their bodies.

King Fobe, aroused by his men, had his men sound the alarm for the rest of the men to gather in the main court. "We are going to hunt these men down like the dogs they are. And this time we will take no prisoners. They all must die!"

As he finished speaking, his men were able to open the fireplace, and like ants coming to the surface, they all poured out of the court and into the tunnel. Fobe's men were very sluggish, though, because not only were they bruised and battered from the previous day's battle, they were also still hung over from the celebration a few hours before.

By now, though, dawn burst forth, and this aided them in their hunt. The Caldans still possessed some of their wolves, for they did not release all of them into the Bendulum forest, so Fobe released them ahead of his men. It was not looking good for Jim and company. You could almost hear Gandalf saying, "Out of the pan, and into the fire."

After riding the waters for several miles, upon hearing the howls of the wolves, Jim and his men exited the river on the opposite side than they entered. That way they would not leave a scent for the wolves to track them. Right now none of the men were armed, and wished they had taken some of the swords that were lying around in the court. Too late for that now.

He survived the battle only to wake up in his own dungeon. Now, he escapes prison only to be chased by wolves. This was the epitome of a bad day.

As the crow flies, they were nearly twenty miles to the coast, but none of them were of a winged species. Besides that, Jim did not want to lead Fobe to where the women and children were, so at one point he led his men west away from the path to the coast.

Fobe knew they crossed over the river at some point, because, when they first released the wolves, they ran straight to the river where the scent died off. Their only chance of catching them was to go downstream and cross over at a shallow point. They jogged along the path for some time until they came to a crossing point, so they forged across, the wolf handlers leading the way, although the wolves were not too keen on submersing themselves in cold water.

Once on the other side of the river, the handlers released them again, so they could pick up on the scent. After some point, the wolves again picked up on the scent, and let loose a number of loud howls to indicate such. Fobe slyly grinned for he knew that his men would soon have Jimban's men trapped.

Jim knew that as well, and at one point stopped the whole company. "Men, there is no way for us to escape, and we cannot lead them to the coast where the women and children are. The only way is for us to set an ambush here in this ravine and face Fobe. Most of us may perish, but that is our only chance of success," he said.

General Corgin spoke up, "What do you have in mind?"

"Well, there is still enough snow in the mountains that we could cause an avalanche. We could gather enough rocks to throw at them from our position, which would entice them towards us. And once they move toward us, we let the snow loose. Hopefully, if we live through it, it will take out Fobe and his men. Then, we can make our way to the coast," Jim explained.

Laedo spoke up, "We have no other choice. I will lead half of the men up the sides of the mountains here to ready the avalanche. The other half will gather what stones you need to ambush them. When you all are ready, everyone shout as loud as you can, and we will let loose the snow."

Jim responded, "Thank you Sir Laedo. Alright men, let's get to it."

This was it. The final showdown. The closing of the curtain. Jim would either defeat Fobe or be defeated by him. There was no other option.

As they positioned themselves on the sides of the ravine, the men gathered as many stones into piles as possible, and, by the time they did, they heard the howls of the wolves nearing their position. It would be difficult for the wolves to approach them at the height they were at on the rocks, but it was not impossible. Thankfully there was enough light out now that they could clearly see any approaching wolves, and could take clear aim at them with their stones and rocks.

The men up top with Laedo were busy pushing trees over on either side of the ravine. Their plan was to get a number of trees pushed over to jostle the snow at the bottom, which would loosen up the snow above it. This, they hoped, would bring the necessary avalanche that Jim and the others planned for. With their trees in place, they awaited the signal from the men in the ravine.

Within a short time, the wolves rounded the corner of the ravine, only to be met with a shower of stones and rocks. There were many yelps and cries from the wolves as they were pounded with stone after stone. Only a handful of them ever got near the men atop their rock fortress. Two of the men were actually attacked by the wolves, and did not survive. The rest of the wolves were either killed or ran away in great pain.

When the wolves made it back to the Caldans, they were bleeding and bruised, Fobe knew that Jim and his men attacked them. Now they were on the lookout, and soon they approached the ravine. As they rounded its corner, they saw some of the carcasses of the wolves lying on the ground, and they knew they were close.

Slowly, they entered the ravine, looking side to side and up in the crags for any signs of the enemy. Jim's men sucked them in enough before they let loose their arsenal of stones and rocks. All at once the sky rained down pain in rounded form. Fobe and his men were all struck at least once, and many of them completely knocked out or killed. They did not let up on the barrage for several minutes, and before they ran out, they all let their voices ring out in a very loud war cry, signaling the men to initiate the avalanche.

Laedo and his men rolled their trees downhill, and that, combined with the men's shouting, shook the snow loose from its sure grip on the mountain. All at once, the snow ran down the mountain, like a herd of wild mustangs descending a great hill, and everyone in the ravine felt its quake rumbling towards them.

Jim yelled out, "Get ready!"

All the men ducked down to prepare for the wave of white death.

Fobe and his men looked up to see their doom approaching, and started to flee back towards the river. When the snow reached Jim's position, it instantly rammed him down the ravine, and within a blink of an eye, cast him upon the back of his arch enemy, Fobe, driving both of them, intertwined, into the freezing, deep waters of the Mattagar.

At that very moment, Jim shot up and out of his hospital bed, soaking wet and absolutely freezing.

Lauren shot up from her chair and was screaming at the top of her lungs, "Ahhhhhhh! Ahhhhh!"

She had no clue what was going on. Jim was standing on the side of his bed near the window in a hospital gown, drenched and half-frozen. Fobe stood between Jim's bed and the bathroom, and he, too, was drenched and half-frozen. Lauren stood there eyeing both of them, still screaming. All of this happened in less than ten seconds. Just as a nurse rushed into the room, Lauren fainted.

Chapter 12 - Unmasking Fear

When the bus hit Jim, he was rushed to Mercy Hospital on the south side of Chicago, and when the avalanche slammed him and Fobe into the Mattagar River, it sent Jim back into his own reality *with* Fobe! Here, the two enemies faced off in a hospital room. Not the most ideal place, but here they were.

As the nurse bolted into the room to see if everyone was alright, Fobe pulled her in, grabbing her and covering her mouth, and shut the door. Jim quickly moved towards Lauren's limp body, which fell back into her chair as she passed out, so that he could place himself between her and Fobe.

"Let her go, Fobe," Jim demanded.

"Heh, heh, heh," Fobe laughed. "All these years you kept coming into my world and escaping. Now, I am in yours. And you know what? There's no escaping!"

Jim responded, "You're wrong, Fobe. Here it's just you and me. You don't have all your goons to help you."

The nurse shook from fear in the arms of Fobe, and tears streamed down the sides of her cheeks. Jim sympathized with her for just a few hours ago he was in the same predicament.

The curtains for the window were open, and Fobe saw that it was dark outside. The nurse he held hostage trembled with fright. Jim was not sure exactly what to do, but he knew he needed to do something. Fobe noticed Jim's agitation, and decided to make the first move. He shoved the nurse very hard towards Jim, hoping to knock him over in the process. Then, as quick as a flash, he turned and ran out of the room.

For a moment, Jim was pinned down by the nurse, so he could not leap after Fobe. The nurse was an emotional wreck, so Jim gently helped her off of him. He ran out of the room to try and catch Fobe. It was too late; he escaped down a fire escape stairwell, and was nowhere to be found.

When Jim ran out of the room, the nurse called security, and within a few minutes, security guards were on scene. They, in turn, called the police and shortly there was an overwhelming presence of law enforcement. By now, Lauren was awake, and was sipping on some tea provided by the nurse. She and the nurse sat on the couch together as the police took their statements. Jim, after changing into a new, dry hospital gown, sat on his bed, still beside himself, as the police tried to get information from him as well.

Once again, Jim found himself in a precarious situation, but this time two other people saw Fobe. The cat was out of the proverbial bag, but he still could not come clean with all the details, at least not with the police. He did not fancy being locked in a looney bin. So he simply told the police that he did not know the man or how he got in his hospital room. He just expressed his gratitude that nobody was hurt. After ten minutes of questioning, the police and security guards left, as well as the nurse, and he and Lauren were left alone. Talk about an awkward situation.

Lauren got up from the couch and sat on the bed next to Jim. She leaned over him and hugged him tightly. Over the past week, she thought she lost him from a bus accident, and then, in some freak situation, she thought she was about to lose him to some mysterious intruder. She had a hard time piecing everything together. Jim just held her as they sat in silence.

As he held her, Lauren finally spoke up, "Jim, who was that man?"

Jim knew that there was no easy answer to this question, so he took a few moments to gather his thoughts before letting any unnecessary words slip out of his mouth. He decided to leave it up to Lauren how much she wanted to know. He asked her, "Do you want to know the truth?"

She sat up, looked into his eyes, trying to weigh his question, and nodded that she did.

Jim thought, "Here goes nothing."

Just as he started to tell her, his family poured into the room, because the nurse had notified them that Jim was awake. Immediately, Lauren sat up from the bed and let his family embrace him.

"Oh my God, Jim! I can't believe you're alive and awake," Anel said as she hugged him. Brent and Mikey came around the other side of the bed and leaned in for hugs as well. John was stationed in Germany at that point, so he was not able to be there. Theresa married after college, and she and her husband were living in North Carolina. Brent and Anel kept her apprised of Jim's situation.

After a couple of hours of visiting, Jim's family left to head home for the night, and he and Lauren were alone once more. That time there was no escaping Lauren's question, and he knew it.

"So you want the truth," Jim said. He looked down and then back up again. Then, he asked her, "Have you ever been absolutely terrified by something in your life?"

"Of course I have," Lauren said.

"Okay," Jim replied then continued, "What were you afraid of?"

Lauren answered, "When I was eight years old, I was at the mall with my mother. She and I were shopping together, having a great time, and at some point I got separated from her. I thought my whole world ended."

"Okay, and how did you react to the situation?" Jim prodded further.

"Well, I remember looking all around me at first to see if I could see her. At that point I really didn't know what to do, so I walked into the nearest store. I walked up to the counter, and told the lady working there I lost my mom," she explained. "But why Jim, what does this have to do with that strange man?"

Jim turned to look out his window and then looked back at her.

"After my father died, my mom got a job to help support us. And a lot of the time John and Theresa were in charge of watching me. One afternoon, exactly one year after my dad died, I went to take a nap. While I slept, my mom went to work, and my brother and sister, thinking they had a couple of hours before I woke up, went to play at their friend's house down the street. The problem was that I woke up before they thought I would," Jim shared.

He continued, "I looked everywhere in our house and was calling loudly for them too. I couldn't find them anywhere. I was six years old at the time and now I was beginning to panic. I didn't know what to do, and I was terrified of being alone. I sat down in the corner of the living, and began to cry."

Lauren, intrigued by what Jim was sharing, asked, "What happened next?"

"Well, what happened next I am not sure how to explain, even to this day. As I sat there crying, the walls of the room all began to shift and move and kind of melt together. That's the best way I can describe it. Then, all of a sudden, an ocean wave splashed me in the face, and when I opened my eyes I found myself on an old sailing, merchant ship," Jim said.

He went on to tell Lauren of his battle with Captain Fobos, and how he escaped. Then, through the middle of the night and early morning, he recalled all his travels to his inner worlds with her.

She sat there with rapt attention, finding it very difficult to believe Jim, yet mesmerized by his tales of battles and adventures.

After some time she spoke up, "So this man that was here is the same man you have been fighting all these years?"

"Yes. He is my fear" Jim said.

Lauren then asked, "Why was he wearing a mask?"

"That," Jim said, "I am not sure." He continued, "Every time I've entered the other worlds, and have battled Fobos, his face has always been covered with a mask. Honestly, it has puzzled me all these years, and now I don't know if I will ever find out."

Lauren still tried to wrap her mind around this whole explanation. She loved Jim very much, and truly wanted to believe him. But the whole thing *did* sound a little kooky. She spoke up, "So, every time these episodes have happened, you went into Fobos' world, right?"

Jim nodded in agreement.

"Then, how did he show up in our world now?"

"I don't know, Lauren," Jim said. He continued, "This last battle was the worst. Almost all of my men were killed. It was the first time he had actually captured me, but then, during the night, we were able to escape into the mountains. King Fobe, uh, Fobos, and his men were after us with wolves. We knew we couldn't outrun them, so we devised a trap. We sucked them into a ravine, attacked them with stones and rocks, and then half of our men let loose an avalanche from the mountains above, sending a torrent of snow cascading down upon us. That wave of snow launched me into Fobos, and threw both of us into the river at the same time. Why do you think both of us were soaked in very cold water when you woke up with him here?" Jim asked.

That last part seemed a little more convincing than the rest of the stories, but all of it was still a hard pill to swallow, especially for someone who had never travelled to these places with him. After several hours of listening, she was exhausted, and soon it would be daylight.

"Jim, I want to believe you, I do, but right now I am so tired. I think we both are. Let's get some sleep, and when you get out of here let's talk about it more," Lauren said.

Jim answered her, "That sounds like a great plan."

With that, she kissed him on the forehead and curled up on the couch with a blanket. Jim let his bed down and within a few minutes was soundly snoring.

They only got about two hours of sleep before Lauren's breakfast showed up, so their sleep was abruptly interrupted. Around eight in the morning the doctor showed up to evaluate Jim.

"Sounds like you two had an eventful night last night," the doctor said.

"Yes sir," they both answered while awkwardly looking at each other.

"Well, Mr. L'Beau, apart from these bruises on your ribs, you seem fine. But I want to run some tests on you before I release you. If everything checks out today, then you will be free to leave this evening. How does that sound?" the doctor asked.

Jim answered, "That sounds great."

Lauren decided to leave for the morning to go get cleaned up and changed. She wanted to take a nap as well, because she was more than tired. "I'll be back this afternoon, and hopefully we can finally bail you out of here."

She gave Jim a kiss on the forehead and left his room. Jim's family showed up around eleven, and brought him lunch. Hamburger and fries with a large chocolate milkshake. Just what the doctor ordered. Or maybe that was just Jim? Either way his stomach was very happy.

After he finished his lunch, the nurse showed up to wheelchair him down to get a CAT scan, because the doctor wanted one more look at his brain before issuing Jim's release. He wanted to be sure his insides matched what he saw on the outside. Within an hour he returned, and within a few hours the results came back positive. Jim was free to go, but for some reason he did not want to. Some urge within himself pulled at him to stay, but he just shrugged it off.

Jim's family said their goodbyes, and parted ways since they parked in a different area than Lauren. Then Lauren and Jim left the hospital together. It was a cool, fall evening, and the sun already set in the west. With all its tall buildings, Chicago got dark quicker than most towns. They entered the parking garage, hand in hand, and walked towards the car.

Just as Lauren helped Jim towards the front passenger seat, Fobe stepped out of the shadows and knocked Jim over the head with a hard object, sending him flying back on his butt. Lauren screamed, and Fobe, at knife point, forced her into the car.

"Give me the keys!" he yelled at her.

She scrambled in her purse, trembling and crying, trying desperately to locate her keys. She grabbed them and handed them to him.

Jim, still lying on the parking lot floor, held his head in pain, and he was completely dazed. Right at the moment he was able to gather his thoughts and realize what just happened, Fobe backed the car up, trying to run Jim over, but he was able to roll out of the way. Then, he sped off down the ramp towards the exit. Fobe was a creation of Jim's mind, and therefore, instantly knew how to do everything he did in Jim's world. Jim jumped to his feet, forgetting all pain at that moment from the adrenaline pulsing through his veins, and went sprinting after the vehicle.

He chased the car out to the road, but was unable to catch them. He could see Lauren through the car windows, and he saw the fear on her face. That cut him to the heart because he knew that his fear now had very real consequences outside his *own* life. Now, it affected the person he was most affectionate about. Just as they escaped his grasp, an elderly woman was approaching her car to get it in. Outside of his character, Jim ran to the woman, and demanded her keys. Frightened, the woman quickly complied, and even tried to offer him her purse as well.

"No thanks," Jim frantically said, as he jumped into the car to continue his chase.

Dual realities were no more for Jim any longer. There was only one reality now, his own. And right now Fobe took over it. Jim was determined to end this incessant battle once and for all that night, but the only problem was he did not know *how* to do it. He did not realize, though, that in a short while their perpetual fight would come to an end, and it would be by Fobe's own hand.

Jim circled the car around quickly, and floored it, avoiding stop signs and stop lights as cautiously as he could. He saw which way Fobe turned, and was pursuing them in the same direction. His best guess was the highway, so he headed straight for it. Driving like a madman, he finally saw Lauren's car in the distance ahead, and this prodded him on even faster.

Fobe saw in his rear-view mirror a car approaching very quickly, driving very erratically, and he perceived this was Jim. This drove Fobe to speed up to an insane speed, as he and Jim weaved in and out of traffic. Then at one point, after several minutes of this high speed highway chase, Fobe abruptly veered off towards an exit, and Jim, trying to avoid hitting another car, could not make the exit.

"Dang it!" he shouted.

He drove near the edge of the highway, and could see where Fobe turned. It seemed as if he was heading towards the port area where the boats and ships were docked.

At the very next exit, Jim turned off and circled back towards the road where he lost Fobe and Lauren. He was singularly focused at that point, like a wolf in pursuit of its prey, and rage-filled anger filled his mind and heart. It was one thing for Fobe to fight against him all these years, but it was another thing altogether for him to apprehend his girlfriend. Fierce determination egged him on.

As Jim sped towards the docks as fast as that old lady's car would go, he heard police sirens ringing out, and he frantically searched for Lauren's car. He knew the police were on their way.

"Where are you, where are you?" Jim said out loud as he looked.

Then, up ahead, he saw her car pulled off to the side by one of the piers, her headlights still beaming. He pulled up right next to the car, almost rear-ending it, and ran around to the front, only to find an empty car with both front doors flung wide open. He looked to his right, and saw the pier lined with very large sailing vessels.

There was no other choice; he had to continue the pursuit on foot.

He was yelling loudly for her, "Lauren….Lauren...Lauren!"

His heart pounded and his palms were completely soaked with sweat from his panicked state of mind. Then thoughts of the worst kind began to invade, "What if he killed her? What if I never see her again?

What do I tell her family? What do I tell my family? How do I explain this?"

"Oh, God, please help me," Jim shot up a quick prayer.

Just then he heard a muffled scream, and instantly recognized the voice. It was Lauren's, so he knew he must be close. He made it towards the last pier, and was going from ship to ship looking at each one. Then, at the end of the pier, he saw what looked like a large sailboat docked, and then he saw that masked-face on the dock, trying to cut the ropes loose as quickly as possible. Just as Jim realized it, Fobe saw Jim at the other end and right at that moment the last rope was cut. Fobe hopped back on the boat, and like a cheetah in pursuit of dinner, Jim took off down the planked pier.

At just that moment, several police cars sped around the corner, and pulled down towards the two abandoned cars. All of the officers jumped out of their vehicles and ran up to investigate at gunpoint the empty cars. As they did, they vaguely saw Jim running towards the end of the dock, and they called in backup from the port. They requested both maritime and helicopter support.

Just as the ship pulled away from the dock, Jim lunged forward with all his might, missing the side of the boat, but he was able to grab the rope, which was trailing in the water, as he plunged into the icy waters of Lake Michigan. Jim held onto the rope for dear life as the boat motored out of the bay. Of course, Fobe had zero regard for rules, and he exited the bay at a very high rate of speed, which made it very difficult for Jim to hold on. Nevertheless he would not relent. Lauren's life depended on it.

Jim knew, though, that he needed to get up the rope and over the side before Fobe made it any farther. The farther the boat got away from the bay area the more difficult it would be for him to stop his enemy. With all his might and strength, Jim pulled himself up the wet rope, burning his hands the whole way, until he reached the edge of the front deck. This whole process proved very difficult for all the obvious reasons, but also because his ribs were still very bruised.

Once he was able to grab onto the deck railing, he edged along the side towards the middle of the ship. He wanted to be as close to the helm as possible before lunging over the side, so he could be close enough to surprise Fobe without putting himself in an awkward position. Fobe had the deck lights on, so he saw Lauren lying down with tape over her mouth with her hands and feet tied, and he could see Fobe standing at the wheel.

As he hung onto the side of the ship, he heard Lauren's muffled screaming, and he heard Fobe talking to her, "Shut up girl, your lover boy is gone. He is back at the dock, swimming around like a drowned rat! It's just you and me, and it's gonna be a long trip. I think I am going to very much enjoy this new world. Ha, ha, ha, ha..."

Jim took this as his cue, and in great pain, pulled himself over the side railing. He quickly got to his feet, and yelled at Fobe, "You're not going to enjoy another minute of this world, Fobe!"

He and Lauren both looked at Jim in great surprise.

"Noooo," Fobe yelled at him, as he ran at Jim. He and Jim collided just as hard as Jim and that bus collided, and both men were determined to end the other's life. Lauren lay there screaming the whole time as she watched the battle unfold between these two arch enemies.

Each man was able to get in a few good punches, but neither could necessarily gain the upper hand. Just as Jim thought he was gaining on Fobe, Fobe reached for a block and tackle, and whacked Jim on the side of the head with it, sending Jim to the floor. Jim lay there, looking towards Lauren, and he saw the fright in her eyes, like a deer staring into the headlights of an oncoming car. He thought that was the end, and he thought he failed.

As he lay there holding his throbbing head, his mind took him back to his first battle with Fobe, and he remembered this was exactly how they first met: on a sailing ship. Then he recalled the advice of Captain Dojure, "Whatever ye do, laddie, stay by me!"

As Jim recalled these words, Fobe leaned over him to wrap some rope around his neck to choke him, and he pulled Jim up to his knees with rope around his neck. He was not able to breathe at all, and he felt his strength failing.

All of a sudden, a helicopter light shined on their ship, and they heard from the loudspeakers, "You on the ship. Halt. You are under arrest."

In that instant, he remembered how bravely Captain Dojure fought on that ship so many years ago, and this thought infused Jim with the strength to fight back. All at once Jim, grabbed the rope around his neck with his hands, stood to his feet, and in the process knocked Fobe in the face with his head, which sent him hurling onto his back.

As Jim leaned over to catch his breath and finish removing the rope from around his neck, he heard the police officers in the helicopter still admonishing them to stop. Lauren looked on with great relief, but knew that Fobe was not dead. And as long as he was not, he still posed a mortal threat to them both. She saw Fobe rising to his feet again and began screaming as loud as she could through her taped mouth. Jim saw her frantic warnings, and turned to face Fobe.

When he did, he yelled at the top of his lungs, "What?!" as he jumped back three feet.

"That's impossible."

Fobe felt his face and realized that his mask was completely cracked and broken, and for the first time Jim saw his face. All these years of fighting Fobe, Jim never saw his face, and it had always been a mystery to him. He never knew why he was never allowed to see his enemy's face when they fought. Lauren froze in complete astonishment.

Then, as the two enemies stood there, finally, face to face, as Jim looked at Fobe, he saw *his own face*. He could not move; he was absolutely stunned. Fear no longer clutched his mind and heart, and his thoughts wandered back over all the years and all of the battles and all the ways that it had seemingly wrecked his life. And now, in an instant, in a singular moment of time, as he recognized fear for what it was, he no longer feared.

Fobe, after feeling his face and realizing that he was unmasked, yelled at Jim, "Come on, fight me! Fight me!"

It was the sound of a person who knew their time was over. As the helicopter light shined on them, Jim looked right at him, and, with a measure of peace he never knew, he said, "No. "It's over, Fobe. I will not fight you anymore, because I no longer fear you."

And with those few poignant words, Fobe dropped to his knees, and, looking upwards, yelled like a wolf howling at moon, "Noooooo!"

As he yelled his last words in Jim's world, just like that, right before Lauren, Jim and the police officer's very eyes, he disappeared. Jim stood there in utter disbelief.

But then, he remembered he needed to untie Lauren. He helped get the tape from off her mouth and the ropes from off her hands and feet. Both of them just sat there and cried together, holding each other very tightly as the moon and stars shone down upon them from the dark sky above.

The officers in the helicopter still belted out commands from the air, and soon the police maritime unit made it to their boat as well. It was all over, and they were both safe. As they sat there, holding each other and gazing into the heavens, Jim took solace in just one thought: fear was no more.

Made in the USA
Columbia, SC
22 April 2019